Embers in the Dark

Dodge Merrin

Paperback ISBN-13: 979-8-9909079-6-6

Cover design by Calley Dunnihoo

Content Warning: *This book contains depictions of science fiction themed violence.*

Contents

Part I
History

Birth of the Knights

Ordeos
Saturday, May 14th, 2242
10:01 A.M.

"Nearly ten years ago, humanity was savagely attacked by a coalition of alien nations, many of whom we once considered friends. They attacked without warning, without provocation, with the intent of enslaving or killing every last man, woman, and child of the human race," Emperor Haiden Lentaise addressed the crowd gathered before him.

People from all walks of life shouted their outrage as he paused to revel at the sight of his loyal subjects spread out over the grassy field, happily foregoing the comforts of home or even an auditorium so they could hear him speak. Ten years ago he was preparing a fight for his people's independence, but hadn't dreamed he would one day be an emperor.

Yet here he was, standing on a stage with his ten most loyal soldiers stretched out on either side of him, all of them attired in full military dress uniform. They'd survived perils beyond imagining to guarantee the safety not only of their own world, but also that of many others who had pledged their loyalty to Ordeos.

"It wasn't long before Earth's military began falling before them and the people they swore to protect were abandoned to their fate. One planet alone did not have the resources to fight off this menace, and when they saw this weakness, more aliens attacked in an escalating frenzy to steal everything we have.

"Then the Earth government finally saw sense and granted independence to all colony worlds, lifting the restrictions against military creation. They barely allowed us a voice in the government, denied us from serving in their military, but now they were looking to us to save the entire human race from their failure."

The crowd shouted and booed its disbelief at this arrogance.

"They didn't know it at the time, but Ordeos was already strong. We knew we couldn't rely on people from a planet on the other side of the galaxy to protect us, and had prepared for the day we would need to defend ourselves. This allowed us to join the fight immediately, and our strength held the line until the other colonies could organize and field their own fighting forces. Many of them chose to join us, and together we created an empire that stands against destruction and chaos.

"The war ended one month ago today with the total defeat of all who threatened us. The entire human race owes its continued existence to Ordeos!"

Cheers erupted, and the crowd began chanting, "Ordeos! Ordeos! Ordeos!"

The emperor allowed them to continue for as long as they wished, basking in the celebration for several minutes.

"On that day, as I gazed upon the last alien world to fall, I vowed I would never allow such a threat to humanity to rise again. I have thought long and hard on how to fulfill this vow, and realized there is only one logical conclusion."

He scanned the crowd carefully, making sure everyone was paying close attention. The flags snapped sharply in the breeze at either end of the stage, leaves rustled in the nearby woods and a few birds flew by overhead, but every eye was set on the emperor with eager anticipation.

"If the safety of the human race is to be guaranteed, it must be the only race to exist. We will wipe out every alien civilization that dared threaten us. We will kill every last one of them and burn their cities to ash. We will scour this galaxy clean and build a new and glorious future."

There was no response from the crowd.

Silence reigned as those present processed his words.

Birdsong could be heard in the woods, carried to them on the breeze.

He watched, and waited, while the people before him remained motionless.

Finally, someone shouted out his response.

"The only good alien is a dead alien!"

Murmurs of agreement passed through the crowd, which then grew into excited whispers, and finally everyone was cheering again.

"Humans first!"

"It's what they deserve!"

"End it forever!"

This continued until Haiden called for silence by raising his arms and stretching them toward the crowd.

"Our brave soldiers stand ready to carry out this task, but a mission of this magnitude requires a degree of dedication, skill, and experience surpassing that of the average soldier and the officers that lead them. To fill this need, I have created the Star Knights, an organization of elite warriors who will lead this fight and see our people through to victory.

"Those standing here with me have distinguished themselves in battle and earned the highest honors any nation has to offer, and they are the first of these new knights. They have sworn fealty directly to me, and have vowed to live their entire lives as warriors in service to the empire. Each and every one of them has fought beside me on the battlefield, and I trust them with my life. When you see them, you see me."

The knights stepped forward in unison to the sound of fervent applause and cheers then snapped right fists to their hearts, saluting the audience in the new style.

Their hearts for the empire.

They completed the salute and stepped back, their faces expressionless despite the crowd's continued exuberance and the emperor's final words.

"To the future!"

8:03 P.M.

"Earth and Vehla have publicly denounced the extermination campaign, but all the others are with us," Darius reported as he walked beside his emperor on the beach. The waves splashed lazily to their left, and the sun set slowly over the ocean to cast a peaceful glow over them.

"We know what must be done, and we have shown everyone the way. If they fail to follow, then they will fade into obscurity," Haiden responded.

He stopped and turned to the right, and Darius followed suit. A little over a mile away, an armada of construction equipment stood silent but ready with mountains of building materials rising up behind them.

"Empires are created with blood, but sustained with faith. While you are out there spilling blood, I will be here creating faith. This city will be the greatest ever built by human hands, and it will be the crown jewel of the empire that finally leads humanity into achieving its full potential," Haiden commented, his eyes growing distant as he peered into the future. Darius looked at the scene before him and tried to picture what his friend was describing, but not even these peaceful surroundings could dim the visions of war, both past and future, raging in his mind.

The emperor turned to look Darius in the eye, and placed a hand on each of his shoulders.

"You have been my closest friend and staunchest ally since I first decided to overthrow Earth's rule. Your ferocity and cunning in battle are without equal, and I know you believe in the cause as much as I do. As such, I have decided to name you as the first Master Knight," he revealed.

"I have followed you because you are able to see the future for what it should be, and you have the cunning and leadership ability to make it happen. It will be my honor to lead the knights in your name," Darius responded, then fell silent as he looked back towards the construction site.

A cool breeze blew in from the ocean as the sun dipped below the horizon, ruffling their hair but not disturbing a single piece of their tight uniforms, but neither man reacted to the dropping temperature as darkness fell about them.

"Speak your mind."

"I cannot see what you see, Haiden. All the death I have seen, all the killing I have done, has destroyed every last semblance of peace within me until all I can see is war. There is no other future for me, but I have no regrets. I gladly go out to eliminate all threats to the future you will build, for I trust you to create a better life not only for our people, but for all mankind."

"For all mankind," Haiden repeated.

Silosan III
Tuesday, August 23rd, 2242
9:03 A.M.

It was hard to believe the planet Darius now viewed from the window in his quarters aboard the carrier Counterstrike had been green and beautiful mere days in the past. Thick, black smoke now obscured most of the surface, and what little could be seen was brown and bare – dead.

He'd personally led every battle in the campaign thus far, but had decided it was time for others to gain the experience to lead and fight without him. They would be expanding the campaign after this, and soon there would be many battles occurring simultaneously.

"Master Knight Pente to the bridge. Urgent."

So much for letting others take care of things this time.

Already in full uniform, the knight took one last look at the planet, then departed for the bridge.

"What is the problem?" he asked upon arriving.

"We managed to cut off and destroy the last of their forces while they were in full retreat, but when we approached the base they were falling back to, our people were stopped by an energy shield. All ground forces in the area have surrounded it, but so far it has held up to everything we've fired on it, including orbital strikes," the captain reported.

"Why wasn't this shield detected when we first arrived?"

"They are masking the energy signature somehow. We still aren't seeing it on sensors. The shape and size you're seeing on tactical was calculated from weapon hits."

"A planetary shield is a difficult undertaking, even for aliens. What could possibly remain that is worth such protection?" Darius mused as he viewed the area on the tactical display. He ordered the captain to send the tactical information to all knights in the fleet, then tapped the comm unit in his ear to open his private command channel.

"All knights, gather a squad of regulars and prepare for debarkation to surface. Target information is coming to you now. Landing coordinates and mission parameters to follow shortly."

Not bothering to wait for a confirmation on his order, the master knight sat at the tactical station to create a plan for getting past the shield and entering the base within.

10:32 A.M.

The din of digging equipment several feet to Darius' left filled the air as it tunneled through the rock, but he ignored it and studied the shield before him. The only indication of its existence was a shimmering and the static charge causing the hair on his uncovered head to stand up.

He removed his right glove and reached out towards the distortion and soon felt the sensation of ants running over his skin, ants which grew angrier the closer he got.

"Careful, sir," a lieutenant commented from behind, but he paid no attention and continued moving his hand closer to the distortion.

The tingling sensation of static electricity changed to burning as if he were within inches of touching a fire and he finally stopped, keeping his hand there for several seconds to familiarize himself with the sensation and committing it to memory.

"We're through."

"The other teams?"

"Awaiting your order to proceed."

The master knight pulled his hand back and replaced his glove while returning to his squad at the mouth of the tunnel.

"All teams, move in," he ordered over his command channel, then led his own unit into the tunnel. Someone asked him if he wanted a rifle, but he shook his head no. It would only get in his way.

They traversed the reddish, rocky ground between the shield perimeter and the base without incident and approached the first building. Once inside, they discovered it to be dark and quiet and Darius realized all the base's power must be going to the shield. They searched the building without encountering any resistance or finding anything of value and the other knights reported similar experiences at their locations.

“Why have a shield protecting an empty base?” one knight commented on their private channel where the regular soldiers couldn't hear.

“Maybe it’s a trap? They knew a planetary shield would catch the attention of our leaders, so they rigged the base to explode once we were lured down here?”

“If that were the case, they wouldn't have masked the shield from our sensors. No, there is something here they didn't want us to find. Keep searching,” Darius ordered.

The next building he came to was a barracks which he expected to find in disarray, but everything was in its place. The beds were made, the kitchen was clean and organized, and the floors were freshly cleaned.

“If this place is so important, why didn't they stay to defend it?” a knight questioned after they all reported in.

“Quit the guessing game and keep looking.”

They made it through nearly the entire base in this manner, finally converging on the last building together, looking at each other dumbfounded.

“Knights, we search this one alone. The rest of you, secure the area,” Darius ordered, then led the six knights inside.

The lights came on the moment they stepped inside, revealing a small room with a booth on one side which had a large window wrapping around it halfway up the wall. Opposite from them was a thick metal door, power sealed shut.

“Finally,” a knight murmured. Another one went up to the door, then reported there was no mechanism for opening it.

“Stand back,” the first knight to speak warned, then slammed the butt of his rifle against the booth window, which resulted in nothing more than a dull thud.

“Huh,” he remarked, then turned to see the others staring at him like he was the dumbest person alive.

“Remind us how you got to be a knight, again?”

"What are you talking about?"

"It's a security booth. Did you really think it would be that easy to break into?"

"Well, when you put it that way."

"Impulsiveness does not befit a knight. Think before acting, and always act deliberately. Maintain discipline at all times," Darius chastised, and the knight in question acknowledged him with a nod before backing up to stand near a wall.

The master knight held out a hand, someone gave him a small explosive, and he placed it on the window. They backed up as far as they could and he detonated it, blasting a hole large enough to reach an arm through.

A knight went up to it, studied the panel underneath it on the other side, then reached through and pressed a button. A buzzer sounded, the door popped open, and the nearest knight pressed himself to the wall with his rifle aimed at the opening. He nodded, and another knight swung the door open the rest of the way.

"Clear."

They hustled through to find themselves in a brightly lit, wide hallway without any doors, but a junction going off to the right could be seen halfway down.

"Can anyone read this?" Darius questioned, referring to a sign on the wall with arrows next to the writing. The only answer was people shaking their heads no.

"Astor, take Quintus and Gerry down the hall to the right. The rest of us will continue forward."

Darius and his team followed the hall until they came to another sealed door at the other end. This one had a number pad on the wall to its right, so one of them took it apart and hacked it while Darius and the other one watched the hall.

When it opened, they found stairs leading up, and at the top there was another door where they had to repeat the process.

Then there was another hallway, this one without any junctions, but in the center on the left they found yet another security door, this one requiring both a code and a retinal scan. This time Darius elected to simply blow it open.

On the other side was a large room filled with desks and computers, and in the center they found an alien in a disheveled dark blue suit sitting on the floor with his back to a desk. When they approached, he looked up at them with fresh tears in his eyes and the remnants of old ones staining his face.

He was mostly humanoid, with two arms and two legs, but was bald, had a bony ridge atop his head going from front to back, and his skin was pale and splotchy.

"Here to finish the job?" he asked in their language.

"What is this place? Why is it protected by a shield?" Darius questioned while using a hand-signal to tell the others to search the room.

"Why do you care? You've destroyed everything else, killed everyone else. Just get on with it already."

Smiling, Darius knelt to rest on his haunches, wrists resting lightly on his knees.

"That's right. We've destroyed everything. You are the last of a dead race, sitting on what is quickly becoming a dead world. Why bother to try and hide this place, or protect it from destruction should it be found?"

"Our leaders thought we would be able to come back one day. They underestimated the depths of your evil."

"We only do what we must to ensure the safety of our people. Now, tell me what is hidden here."

"You are going to kill me one way or the other, so why should I bother to answer your questions? Even if you should happen to let me live, I don't have anything left to live for."

Sighing, Darius stood up and drew his pistol.

"Yes, I am going to kill you. The method of your death I leave to you," he threatened, then took aim at the alien's left knee.

"We have something here!" Astor's excited voice came over the comm.

"What is it?" Darius questioned while keeping his eyes and gun on the alien.

"We found a fully stocked armory next to a lab. It looks like this was a research station."

"Seal both rooms and get back to the soldiers outside."

"I don't understand."

"Understanding is not required. Obey my order."

"Yes, sir," Astor replied sullenly, and Darius lowered his pistol just far enough to point at the floor.

"Why didn't you destroy this place yourselves?" he questioned.

"Our government didn't want to, but the last of us decided to do it anyway after you killed all our leaders. You stopped the last of the military before they could get here, and I don't have the means to do it myself."

Darius nodded, then shot the alien in the head.

2:47 P.M.

"Give me a channel to all personnel," Darius ordered once he stepped on the Counterstrike's bridge without slowing his pace as he walked to the captain's chair.

Seeing the look on the knight's face, the captain quickly left his seat and relayed the order to his crew.

"This is Master Knight Pente to all personnel involved in the attack on Silosan III. You are hereby ordered into absolute silence regarding your time here. No matter how insignificant you may think something is, you will not tell anyone about what you have seen and done here.

Violations of this order will be investigated and punished by the Star Knights personally."

He signaled for the channel to be cut, appreciating the look of sudden fear in the eyes of the bridge crew. They would do as they were told.

"Get me a secure channel to the emperor, urgent priority. I'll take it in my quarters," he ordered, then quickly left the bridge.

The aliens were unable to use what he had just found to save themselves, but what they had left behind would ensure the empire's dominance for decades, possibly even centuries.

Now no one could threaten their people, or their dreams, ever again.

Freedom's Twilight

Thursday, February 7th, 2278
3:03 P.M.

The knight dug his hands into ground turned to mud by the melting snow as he slid backward, managing to stop and roll aside just in time to avoid another attack from the creature, then he kicked up and struck it in the side.

His opponent doubled over in pain and screamed in rage as he stood up, after which he punched it in the face and knocked it unconscious.

He took a deep breath and started looking for a weapon so he could finish it off, but was tackled to the ground before he could find anything.

"How many of you are there!"

The alien shouted something incomprehensible from its position on top of him, then lifted him up and slammed him back into the ground.

He scooped up a handful of mud and slung it into its eyes, then pushed it off him when it reared back to wipe it off.

This time when the knight regained his feet, he saw several aliens lined up before him. His attacker, still wiping its eyes, stumbled towards them as they slowly advanced.

He quickly scanned the area around him for any help, but his soldiers lay scattered about the hillside, unmoving, and there wasn't a weapon anywhere near.

They drew closer, clearly wishing to savor the kill, and he slowly backed up until he could feel the heat from the still burning transport behind him.

"Let's get this over with," he grunted, then crouched into a fighting stance.

Three of them charged at once, so he dodged to the right, grabbed that enemy, then spun it around and shoved it into the flames after which it ran away screaming.

The next one grabbed his jacket and pulled him into a headbutt, then tossed him to the ground where his buddy delivered a solid kick to his ribs. Pain shot through him, but he grit his teeth and stayed focused on the fight.

It pulled back for another kick, but he grabbed its foot and pulled, sending it sprawling backward into the muck. He tried to get back on his feet, but the other one jumped on top of him and slammed him down, its hands around his throat.

He gripped its wrists tight and pulled back, but it proved too strong for him. His vision grew blurry, his head pounded, and his grip began to loosen.

Then the pressure suddenly disappeared and he instinctively grabbed his throat and coughed several times as the creature was lifted off him.

He looked to the side to see someone holding his would be killer in the air with one hand while looking down at him with a mildly amused expression.

"I never thought the day would come when I would be rescuing a Star Knight," his rescuer commented, who then stabbed the alien in the gut before tossing it aside.

"Well, it is a good way to be nominated to be trained as a knight yourself," Xavier rasped as he stood up. The other man didn't offer him a hand up, and he didn't ask for one.

He clenched his jaw against the pounding in his head and pain in his side, and looked around to see a squad of short, heavily muscled imperial soldiers securing the area.

"Riken Tenoch, first Nosine Star Knight. I like the sound of that."

"What's our status?"

"Six transports were shot down, including yours, but the rest were able to land and discharge their passengers. There are still some holdouts, but the area is under our control. Command reports that this region is now secure."

"And the planet?"

"One region remains contested, but it will be ours soon."

"Let's get back to base."

3:56 P.M.

"Orders received and understood," Xavier said via the comm unit inside his right ear, then started down the transport ramp with Riken at his side. "Rotate out our field units with the reserves. They are to get some rest, then be ready to go again by nineteen hundred," he ordered the colonel.

"Yes, Knight Captain," Riken responded, then relayed the orders via his own comm unit.

"You will fight what you are told, and when you are told!" someone shouted, and the two of them turned in unison to see another knight glaring down at a Nosine soldier.

"We are not mindless weapons to be thrown at an enemy no matter the consequences!"

"You are imperial soldiers, and you will maintain discipline!"

"Then where is the rest of the army! We are always on the front lines while everyone else sits back and watches!"

"That is the role the emperor has assigned you, and it's time you acted with the respect and honor that entails!"

"Is there a problem here?" Xavier questioned, having approached them unseen while they argued.

"Our invasion was put in jeopardy when this Nosine and his unit refused to attack when ordered. They only obeyed after I called in another unit to replace them."

"You ordered us to attack an enemy stronghold without support!"

"That was the strategy laid out by the knight commander, and it is not your place to question it!"

"Those strategies continually order my people into slaughters!"

"Enough!" Xavier interrupted.

"In short, it's yet another example of Nosine disloyalty," the knight concluded as he glowered at his subordinate.

"We are not disloyal, but we are tired of being the only ones in the line of fire."

"This argument has been rendered academic. I just received orders recalling all the elite Nosine legions back to their homeworld. Fresh legions of regulars are on their way to replace them," Xavier explained.

"Are we ending the campaigns, sir?" Riken asked.

"Never. This is merely another step on the journey to ensure the safety of all humanity," Xavier assured him, then to the others he said, "Now I suggest you stop arguing and get your people ready to move out."

4:11 P.M.

"Well, what are you waiting for?" Riken asked his fellow Nosine after the knights left.

“I don't like this. Something is going on,” Wolfken responded as he glared suspiciously at the backs of the knights. He didn't turn away until after they disappeared inside the camp's command center.

“You're getting exactly what you want, yet you still manage to complain about it. Aren't you ever happy?” Riken observed, then turned to walk away but was stopped by a hand on his arm.

“You're telling me you don't find this the least bit suspicious? Why would they recall *all* the Nosine legions?”

“For the exact reason you were just shouting about. We have been on the front lines for a long time and they are rotating us back to take leave.”

“All of us? There are still a lot of aliens to kill, and they've made a big deal out of using our natural strength as their primary weapon.”

“The next target is probably weaker than those we've been facing, meaning the regulars are more than capable of taking care of them without us. Now stop overthinking everything and get back to work.”

Ordeos

Royal Palace

Tuesday, February 19th, 2278

6:58 A.M.

“Knight Captain Darzin, you're the last to arrive. Take a seat and we'll begin,” Master Knight Traze instructed.

Five other knight captains were also present, each one a commander of the six elite Nosine legions. It was odd for all of them to be present at the same briefing, but Xavier didn't think much of it as he took a seat near the end of the table.

“The increasing number of incidents regarding discipline among the Nosines has caught the emperor's attention and he feels the situation cannot be tolerated any longer," Traze announced, catching Xavier by surprise.

"What incidents? I haven't noticed anything out of the ordinary."

"You saw one of them disputing my orders just the other day!" Venel reminded him.

"Disagreements happen now and then, especially after you have been on the front lines as long as we have."

"All of us have experienced similar problems in recent months, and it is getting worse. Insubordination among the Nosines is on the rise and is bordering on treason," another knight commented.

"I haven't received any insubordination from my soldiers. Perhaps there is something *you* are doing wrong," Xavier challenged.

"That's enough! We are not here to debate whether or not this is happening, we are here to execute the emperor's wishes on the matter," Traze interrupted.

"He's already made a decision?"

"He has. The Nosines have always been a proudly independent people, and they only joined the empire because the aliens were breathing down our necks. Now that we are well on our way to permanently ending the alien threat, Emperor Haiden fears the Nosines are preparing to rebel."

"They wouldn't do that," Xavier argued.

"It doesn't matter. We can't take the risk of a system that close to Ordeos becoming independent," Venel suggested.

"That is the emperor's thinking, and I agree with him. Six fully-equipped legions can do a lot of damage, possibly even enough to jeopardize the extermination campaigns and destroy all we have accomplished," Traze added.

"What has the emperor decided to do?"

"All of the elite legions are to be decommissioned, and the soldiers discharged from service. All Nosines are permanently banned from military service, and new jobs will be found for them in the private sector, starting with heavy labor positions where their strength can be put to the most use."

"That sounds a lot like slavery to me."

"Nonsense. They will be paid fair wages and can choose their jobs just like anyone else, but the emperor wants them out of the military. We will incentivize them to take the jobs we want by offering higher wages and better benefits, but they will not be forced into anything," Traze insisted.

The knight captains glanced at each other, and even Venel appeared somewhat uneasy at this news. Slavery in any form was meant to be a thing of the distant past, disappearing into the mists of time just like Earth. No one wanted to risk bringing it back, but neither did they want to risk the destruction of all they had built, nor was there any disputing the emperor's command.

"When do we start?"

"Immediately."

Nosin
Dovlik City
Thursday, March 14th, 2278
1:17 P.M.

The doors to the imperial discharge office were in constant motion as men and women entered and exited, but to Riken they seemed to be an impassable barrier. He had sought to prevent this in every way he knew how, had even gone so far as to request an audience with the emperor, but all his efforts were in vain.

The decision had been made. No Nosine was to serve in the imperial military, and now they had to live with it.

His only hope to fight against the alien menace now lay with Knight Captain Darzin's promise to make him a Star Knight. Despite the decree, he vowed to continue his efforts in making that happen.

Most of the freshly discharged soldiers exiting the building were smiling, happy to be home with no obligation to face the horrors of war ever again, but a few walked away with anger or tears in their eyes. They believed in this fight and wanted to do their part, but were now forbidden to do so thanks to the actions of a few.

He sighed, then finally crossed the street and entered the building.

"That's it?" he heard someone exclaim before the doors could even close behind him.

The entrance led to one large room filled with lines leading up to ten service windows, one of which had an angry Wolfken waving a credit voucher in the air.

Of course *he* would be causing a scene.

The clerk said something Riken was unable to hear, so he began threading his way through the crowd to where he could keep a closer eye on the situation. Most of the other soldiers knew him and his likely motives, and as such did not protest as he moved ahead of them in the line.

"This cannot be all my backpay! I have been on the frontlines for months, and am owed combat pay!"

"I gave you what your records indicate you are owed. If there is a problem, then you need to contact your superior officer."

"I am a legion commander, and I demand you give me what I am owed!"

"You *were* a legion commander. Now step aside before I have you arrested," the clerk threatened, causing Wolfken to reach out and grab him by the collar.

"Listen here you little..."

Several people, including Riken, moved in to intervene, but froze solid when a gunshot rang out.

Silence fell.

Time seemed to slow to a crawl.

The clerk fell back into his chair.

And Wolfken slowly slid to the floor, where he stayed – unmoving.

Riken knelt beside the body, checked for a pulse, and found nothing. He carefully turned his fellow soldier onto his back and respectfully closed his eyes. Two pairs of Ordonian military boots took up position on either side of him while whispers slowly spread through the crowd at his back.

"You didn't have to kill him."

"He was attacking an imperial officer."

"We were right here and were about to stop him. You could have let us take care of it, or you could have wounded him, but you deliberately aimed for a kill shot."

"I wasn't about to take any chances with someone twice as strong as his victim or myself."

The whispers grew more intense, and the guards looked around the room as if seeing the onlookers for the first time. Frantic rustling added to the noise as others sought to move to the front, and Riken slowly rose to his feet where he noticed all the guards move their rifles away from their chests and halfway to an aiming position.

"There's nothing more to see here. Get back in line and let's get this business over with," the guard Riken had been speaking to commanded, but no one moved.

"Wolfken!"

A particularly burly Nosine burst out of the crowd and ran up to the body where he stood with fists clenched and his body shaking.

"I said, get back in line," the guard threatened, and pointed his rifle at the new offender.

"There's no need for that," Riken stated as he moved to stand between the two, but the Nosine shoved him aside before batting the weapon away and seizing the guard with both hands.

The other guard took aim, but Riken grabbed his gun in time to redirect his shots into the ceiling. He proceeded to disarm him, then took a step back, but before either of them could do anything else several more Nosines descended on the man.

He tossed the rifle aside and attempted to pull them off him, but it was too late.

The remaining guards began firing randomly into the crowd, and people ran in all directions as screams of pain and rage filled the air.

"Stop! We are not enemies!" Riken yelled at the top of his lungs as he backed away from the epicenter, but it was to no avail. Even if anyone could hear him, they were beyond listening.

A few guards waded into the crowd, attempting to reach their friends, but they were quickly overwhelmed by the Nosines and taken down.

Now equipped with weapons of their own, the former soldiers turned and opened fire on the Ordonians.

Someone crashed into Riken and he stumbled sideways, then slipped in something and fell to the floor. He felt something sticky on his hands and held them up to find them dripping red, then looked around to find the floor covered in the thick substance now filling the air with a metallic stench.

He screamed and stumbled to his feet, then ran towards the front, plowing through anyone who got in his way.

He reached the entrance as a soldier was entering, and was rewarded with a rifle butt to the face which sent him back to the floor where he found himself staring into the wide, unblinking eyes of a guard.

More Nosines reached the door, and fought back the Ordonian reinforcements before spilling out into the street.

Combatants ran past, with many stepping on him, but Riken hardly noticed as he reached out and closed the man's eyes which would be forever open in his memory.

Fort Jalvik
2:02 P.M.

Men and women pulled on remaining pieces of uniforms or equipment as they ran to their stations, alarms blaring throughout the base. Xavier ran with them, and was almost to the airfield when he encountered another knight.

"How did this happen?" he demanded.

"Details are scarce, Knight Captain. All we know is that a riot broke out at the discharge center and has spread into the streets. The Nosines are attacking any Ordonians they find, military and civilian."

Xavier cursed under his breath, then ran onto the airfield and climbed aboard the first attack flyer he came across.

"Take me to the riot zone!" he shouted, donning a headset to be heard above the roar of the twin rotors.

"We haven't received takeoff clearance yet, sir!"

"I'm a knight! My orders are all the clearance you need! Take me there now!"

"Yes, sir!"

The craft rose into the sky, then turned towards the capital silhouetted in the distance.

Within minutes they were passing the outskirts where they saw multitudes of vehicles fleeing the city while emergency workers hurriedly erected barricades on the streets to protect homes and businesses.

"There! Take us to that smoke," Xavier pointed from within the cockpit, then he went to the middle section where he took over a side-gunner position.

Seconds later they were flying over streets swarming with short-statured Nosines toppling vehicles, smashing windows, and setting fires. Xavier fired at a group rushing towards a car with a family inside, but only targeted the ground between them.

It stopped them long enough for the driver to turn around and drive off, but it didn't stop them entirely. They searched for the source of the gunshots, and upon finding it, returned fire. Rail accelerated bullets pinged off the armored hull, but caused no damage.

"We should take them out, sir!"

"Negative. These are imperial citizens, and I will not kill them!"

"They are a confirmed threat to other citizens, sir! We need to stop them!"

"No! Hold fire!"

"Sir..."

"I said hold your fire!"

They couldn't simply slaughter hundreds of their own people. There had to be another way.

The issue was decided for him when a general broadcast came over the comline.

"This is a direct order from Emperor Haiden Lentaise. All emergency forces are to vacate the riot zone and military forces are to leave the city immediately."

The pilot looked back at Xavier expectantly, and he nodded to confirm the order.

He fixed his gaze behind them, his jaw clenched in grim anticipation. He didn't like where this was going.

Dovlik City
2:43 P.M.

"Oh, no!" Riken's wife Leticia gasped as he stumbled through the front door of their house near the edge of the city.

"It isn't mine," he reassured her as he glanced at the blood dripping on the floor.

"But your head," she observed, reaching out towards his face.

"I've had worse," he responded, smiling weakly in an attempt to calm her. Her concern didn't fade, but she gathered herself together and helped him sit on the entryway bench before disappearing into the kitchen.

"What happened? I heard there was a riot at the discharge office," she asked upon returning with a damp towel with which she proceeded to clean his face.

"Someone got mad and grabbed a clerk because he thought he wasn't getting his fair pay. A guard shot and killed him, and it all blew up from there."

"Mommy! Daddy!" a child's voice cried from the front yard, and they darted outside to find their daughter pointing towards the sky.

"What is that?" Leticia asked as she grasped the front of her husband's shirt.

"A railgun shot fired from a ship."

The projectile slammed into the city district where Riken had been little more than an hour ago, and flames burst into the sky as the ground quaked beneath them.

The shockwave had barely subsided when a small ship positioned itself above the city where it broadcast a message loud enough to be heard for miles.

"Rebellion will not be tolerated! You are ordered to put down your weapons and submit to imperial investigation! Resistance will be severely punished!"

An eerie silence fell as the ship disappeared back into the sky. Fresh explosions continued in and around the bomb site as clouds of smoke began to block the sun, but around them all was calm.

"What happens now?" Leticia asked softly.

"The same thing that happens every time a government forces its will on people using violence.

"Revolution."

Dawn of Tyranny

Nosin
Thursday, April 3rd, 2279
1:03 A.M.

The starless night shone no light on the man in combat fatigues as he made his way up the cliff path, mirroring the darkness within his soul, but his steps did not falter on the uneven ground.

How had it come to this? Friends once united in common cause were now intent on destroying one another. Their mutual enemy remained undefeated, yet for months they poured their energy into fighting amongst themselves, and there was no end in sight for either conflict.

The path leveled out and he continued along the cliff face for a few meters.

"Not the place I'd expect to find someone out on a morning stroll," a voice challenged from ahead of him.

"A simple stroll is not enough to relieve my burden," Riken Tenoch responded with the code phrase and the guard let him pass.

He placed his left hand on the rough stone and felt along it while he walked, then stopped and turned when it slid off into open air. A damp chill greeted him as he proceeded forward and he proceeded slowly, counting steps as he went. When he reached twenty, he turned to the right and reached forward until he felt some hanging fabric which he then pushed aside to reveal a soft yellow glow.

He quickly passed through, making sure the heavy strips closed completely behind him, then continued deeper into the cave lit by portable lanterns. A guard at the first T-intersection greeted him with a nod as he turned left and headed towards a large chamber. A few rebels sat on either side of the passage with their gear, but none of them looked up and he didn't attempt conversation.

Upon entering the main chamber he discovered a couple dozen men, women, and children situated around the edges lying on simple mats or sitting nearby. Some were sleeping, but most busied themselves with whatever they could get their hands on, unable to rest with the burden on their minds and hearts.

Riken passed through the chamber and another series of tunnels on the other side until he found a much smaller room with a solitary man leaning over a wooden table staring at a map. He was dressed in camouflage as was Riken, neither of whose outfits had been washed in quite some time. Creation and maintenance of proper uniforms was a luxury they couldn't afford currently.

“I hope you bring good news for me, Riken.”

“I'm not sure there is any such thing anymore, Avson,” Riken responded, and the other man sighed before pushing off from the table and giving his guest a hug.

“I'll settle for you not telling me that someone has died,” Avson said after letting go.

“Nobody that I know about. The Ordonians have actually pulled back to fortify their positions.”

“Why would they do that? Surely they're not expecting a counterattack?”

“Unknown. We haven't been making things easy for them, but they were making steady progress against us. There's no reason for them to stop now.”

“Perhaps their position is weaker than we thought?”

“I don't see how it could be, but I suppose it's possible.”

"Perhaps we should launch a new offensive, striking them before they can finish shoring up their defenses?" Avson suggested.

"I'm not sure that's a good idea. It could be exactly what they want, luring us into some sort of ambush to thin out our numbers," Riken advised.

"You're right. We don't have enough information to risk what few resources we have, but if something doesn't change soon, we're all dead anyway."

"All we can do for now is to resist the best way we can until we find some advantage. Either way, Ordeos can't fight two wars forever," Riken reassured him.

"To think that we fought and died for them for so long," Avson mused. Riken clapped a hand on his shoulder and the two of them shared a commiserate smile.

"I need to check on my wife and daughter and try to get some sleep. You should do the same. Maybe fresh eyes are what we need to find a solution," Riken told him, and the other commander nodded wearily as he looked at the map.

Ordeos
Royal Palace
8:00 A.M.

The knight captain entered the conference room to find it empty save for one man standing at the head of the table covered in documents and tablets.

"Knight Captain Xavier Darzin, reporting as ordered, sir," he announced and saluted with his right fist over heart.

"Approach," Master Knight Traze responded without looking up or returning the salute.

Xavier walked up to stand beside him and glanced at the paperwork to discover that it was all related to the Nosine rebellion.

"This ridiculous insurrection has gone on far too long. It must end," Traze declared.

An insurrection which began because of the paranoid actions of people in the government and military, but Xavier decided not to mention that fact.

"We have managed to prevent our enemies and allies from learning about this mess, but it is only a matter of time before they do. If they sense weakness, everything will be lost," Traze expounded.

The master knight finally looked up from the documents and into the eyes of his subordinate.

"That must not be allowed to happen. The emperor has charged Crown Prince Razis with ending the Nosine Rebellion as quickly as possible, and he has recalled all our forces engaged against the aliens."

"We shouldn't halt the campaign merely to deal with a relatively small internal matter. The aliens will use it as an opportunity to fortify their positions and possibly even launch a new offensive against us," Xavier objected.

"The next alien race is weak enough that Tadavin can handle them without our help. We've told them we are granting our soldiers some much needed leave, but we'll actually be using them to storm Nosin and establish order."

"I understand, sir. What are my orders?"

"You are to take your legion and subdue the Javai region, the area with the most rebel activity. There are no rules of engagement here. Do whatever is necessary to get the job done."

"Understood."

Nosin
Monday, April 7th, 2279
2:03 P.M.

"Exactly what we need. Thank you," Riken told the older woman standing on his left. He and eighteen other rebels were behind her store inspecting several crates of food sitting on the ground, all of them in faded civilian clothes of various colors.

"I only wish I could do more," the woman responded.

"You do far more than anyone could ever ask, Huvia. We would have starved to death by now if it wasn't for you," Riken assured her, then told his people to begin loading the crates in the truck. When they were finished, he would leave in the truck with another soldier while the others made their way back to camp with the rest of the supplies by other means.

A scream suddenly split the quiet afternoon air, freezing them all in place.

"That came from up the street," Huvia observed, then rushed into her shop.

"Hurry and finish loading," Riken ordered his soldiers, then followed their supplier. He clenched his jaw as possible reasons for the scream raced through his mind, knotting his stomach in the process.

He went through the shop and emerged from the front to find several Ordonian soldiers escorting a tank down the street going through the center of town. Townspeople ran and hid anywhere they could, all except for one who confidently walked up to the captain at the head of the formation.

The captain held up a hand to signal a halt and allowed the man to approach him. They talked for a moment, then the man turned and pointed towards the shop in front of which Riken and the old woman still stood.

"Not good," Riken muttered as he locked eyes with the informant who then turned and ran.

When he saw the Ordonian captain turn to signal his troops, Riken grabbed Huvia's arm and pulled her back into the store. They were barely out the back door when he heard the tank fire, and he pulled her to the ground as an explosion ripped through the building.

"Take her in the truck and get out of here!" he shouted. Three rebels jumped into the back of the half-full pickup truck while another grabbed the store owner and shoved her into the passenger seat.

"What about you?" he asked after slamming the door.

"Go!" Riken shouted.

"Look out!"

There was a gunshot, and Riken turned back towards the shop to see an Ordonian falling down beside the building.

"Retreat!" he ordered as the truck peeled out behind him, then led the rest of his rebels in the opposite direction. One of them fell beside Riken as the rest of the soldiers emerged and opened fire, but he didn't slow down.

They kept running behind the buildings until an enemy jeep cut them off, forcing them to turn left down an alley where they found themselves facing three soldiers, but they kept running.

Four of them fell when the soldiers opened fire, but the rest closed the distance, disarmed the soldiers, and knocked them to the ground before continuing forward.

Now out of the alley and on the main street, there was the tank to contend with. It fired it's main cannon at them, but missed and destroyed a nearby house instead.

"We can't escape!"

The group paused at the alley's opening while the tank zeroed in on them, but it didn't fire. Instead, the soldiers escorting it rushed forward in expectation of their imminent surrender.

Then Riken heard an engine from behind and turned to see the jeep from earlier coming up the alley, but it screeched to a halt to avoid hitting the unconscious soldiers lying between them.

"We're not done yet," he said, then charged the jeep.

The group swarmed over it before its occupants could react and pulled everyone out. Riken slid in behind the wheel, threw it in reverse, then floored it.

Upon exiting the alley, he put it in forward gear, then cut through a parking lot to connect with the street on the other side which he then followed out of town.

Friday, April 11th, 2279
12:32 A.M.

"The Ordeon Empire exists to protect the people and build the future. We cannot allow anyone or anything to threaten that purpose, including people we once called friends. The rebels chose their own personal pride over the greater good of all people, and they must be stopped. You can help me do that," Xavier explained as he walked around the man tied to the chair in the center of the room.

A single fixture dangled above the chair, casting a dim light over the prisoner whose face was currently obscured by his long unkempt hair as he let his head hang down.

"I just want to go home," he whimpered.

"Tell me where I can find the rebels."

"But they're fighting for our freedom."

"You are already free citizens of the Ordeon Empire. The rebels fight only for their own pride."

The knight stopped in front of the crying man, and knelt down to his level.

"What was Nosin like before the rebellion?"

The prisoner didn't respond.

"What was your life like? Did you ever want for food? For a job?"

"No."

"Did you feel safe?"

"Yes."

"Is it like that now?"

"No."

"Why did it change?"

"I don't know."

"*When* did it change?"

No response.

"It can be that way again. The empire is here to create a safe and prosperous future for all humanity. Don't let selfish, greedy, ignorant people delay that future," Xavier encouraged.

He waited as the man slowly stopped crying, then looked up and met his eyes.

"I'll tell you everything I know."

Rebel Cave
9:03 P.M.

"I'm surprised she's able to sleep down here," Riken commented to his wife as they gazed at their daughter lying on a mat.

"At her age, it doesn't take long for something to become normal. She probably doesn't even remember what a real bed feels like," Leticia responded.

"That's no small mercy," Riken observed as he massaged his right shoulder.

"We'll get through this. Not even a paranoid emperor can keep us down for long."

A sudden shaking interrupted Riken's response, and the girl woke up screaming as it grew in intensity.

Both parents grabbed their daughter and covered her with their own bodies as rocks fell from the ceiling and crashed to the floor around them.

When the quaking finally stopped, he let go of his family who continued hugging tight as he grabbed his comlink and demanded an update.

"It was a bombing run! Ordonian troops coming up the path now!"

Cursing, he grabbed his rifle, told his wife and daughter to stay together, and rushed out of the chamber.

"There's no time for that! We have to get to the entrance!" he shouted at some rebels digging at rubble. They fell in behind him, and they gathered anyone else they saw as they rushed through the caves.

The sounds of echoing gunfire greeted them long before they reached the entrance tunnel, and they poured into it to find that the Ordonians had already made it past the shield flaps and were pushing forward.

Yelling, he charged the intruders and plowed into them, tossing them aside like ragdolls. Other rebels joined him, and together they managed to push their attackers back into the first cave.

He dropped his rifle and grabbed a fleeing soldier with both hands, then raised him up and threw him into a wall.

"Don't let them pull back! We have the advantage as long as they can't get range on us!" he called out.

The Nosines dispersed into the enemy ranks with some even making it all the way to the cave opening, but no matter how many soldiers they stopped, more kept coming.

9:47 P.M.

"They're falling back! Push forward!" Xavier shouted, then drew his pistol and led the charge against the retreating rebels. The higher gravity made it feel like he was running underwater, but he gave it everything he had and kept pace with the Nosines as they ran down the first passage.

The tunnel split to both sides, and Xavier took position between at the fork long enough to split his force in half and send one down the right passage while he led the rest to the left.

Several meters later they emerged into a large chamber where the rebels had formed a skirmish line to meet them. When they didn't immediately open fire, Xavier held up his right hand to signal a halt to his troops.

One rebel stepped forward, and the two of them locked eyes in recognition. The pain of betrayal filled his old friend's eyes, and Xavier imagined a similar expression existed on his own face.

"It's over, Riken. Surrender and put an end to this insanity," he advised.

"The emperor would see us become slaves, but we won't allow that."

"You have a family. The career you once had is gone, but don't throw away what you have left."

"I fight for them and all my people."

"We won't allow anything to get in the way of the future we're building," Xavier threatened.

"Then I guess there's nothing left to talk about," Riken responded, then quickly raised his arms and pointed to each side of the Ordonians.

Several Nosines jumped out of cracks in the walls and fell upon the soldiers, easily overpowering those they encountered.

The rebels in the center of the chamber rushed forward at the same time, and Xavier managed to shoot one before having to dodge to the side to avoid being grabbed.

He shot another one, but then the gun was knocked out of his hand and he had to step back to avoid a punch aimed at his face.

Another punch followed, but he dodged it by diving to the side and going into a roll during which he drew his knife. He came out of the roll in a crouching position and threw the knife at his attacker, only to discover it was Riken when it embedded in his chest.

The rebel fell on his side, coughing and choking. His eyes met Xavier's one last time within which he saw nothing but sadness, then turned towards the cave wall as he exhaled one last time.

The knight turned back towards the others expecting another fight, but saw that the other half of his troops had shown up and gunned down the rebels.

"That appears to be all of them, Knight Captain. A few of us rushed ahead through the tunnel on the other side of this chamber, but they report finding only non-combatants," a lieutenant reported.

The knight looked towards where he was pointing to see some of his troops leading women, children, and elderly out of a tunnel and corralling them in the center of the chamber.

"Daddy!" a little girl screamed, then tore her hand from her mother's and ran to Riken's body.

Her mother followed, making no sound even as tears flowed down her face. A soldier moved in to intercept them both, but Xavier waved him off and watched as the girl buried her face in Riken's chest and the woman fell to her knees beside them both.

He couldn't afford to show his own sorrow at the death of his old friend, not in front of his soldiers who only saw the man as a rebel, but he did whisper one thought.

"The price of the future."

Darkened Justice

Nosin
Dovlik City Postal Service
Tuesday, June 3rd, 2313
9:02 A.M.

"All I want to do is send a package to my son!" Sanjic exclaimed.

"No mail of any kind is to be sent off-world without the express approval of the governor," the Ordonian clerk insisted from behind a protective screen.

"I have to get the governor's approval to send something to my own son?"

"That's correct. Is there something else I can help you with today?"

"Yeah, call the governor and get that approval."

"That is outside my jurisdiction. You should leave if there is nothing else."

The forty-eight year old man sighed, laid a hand on the small package sitting on the counter, and looked the young woman directly in the eyes.

"Look, this is my son's first time working on another planet. I just want to send a little something to remind him of home. Does it really need to be so complicated," he pleaded.

She began to respond, but then her eyes darted to his right at the same time he heard the whine of a hydraulic motor.

"Is there a problem here?" a deep voice asked, and Sanjic turned to see an Ordonian cop with movement assistance machines attached to his arms, legs, and back.

"He wants to send a package offworld," the clerk explained.

"You know the rules. All communications coming to or from Nosin are strictly regulated by the government. If you have no other business, leave."

There wasn't anything he could do, so Sanjic grabbed his package and walked back through the lobby while ignoring the looks of sympathy or resentment he received from his fellow Nosines.

Imperial Courthouse
10:22 A.M.

"This is our last chance," Ninal mused as she stared at the heavy wooden door leading to the judge's office.

"We can always petition the authorities on Ordeos next," her husband Cyvin suggested with a glance at their attorney for confirmation, but he just looked away.

"They'll never listen to us."

"We can't stop trying. Your father is a hero, and deserves to be remembered as such. We will see to that, one way or another," Cyvin responded. She shot him a look to warn him to be more careful, then glanced at the Ordonian secretary sitting behind her desk a few feet from them, but she showed no reaction to his words.

"There is a lot of work to be done," Ninal consented.

"Judge Nezin will see you now," the secretary announced as she rose to open the door for them. Ninal and Cyvin both took a deep breath, then stood and followed their attorney into the office where they found a heavyset man in flowing black robes sitting behind a large wooden desk.

“Sit,” he commanded, and the couple each took a seat in one of the four chairs facing the desk, but their lawyer chose to remain standing.

“Thank you for seeing us, Your Honor,” the lawyer greeted, but Nezin ignored the formality.

“I have read your petition and understand you seek to repeal the status of Traitor to the Empire as it applies to Riken Tenoch, but the petition failed to specify any new information to justify this action.”

“Riken Tenoch was an accomplished officer in the emperor's army who was in the process of being considered admission to the Star Knights when he found himself in the midst of extraordinary circumstances,” the lawyer replied.

“At which time he chose to take up arms against his lawful government. How does that not make him a traitor?”

“He felt there was a need to defend himself and others, so he did exactly what he was trained to do.”

“As did the loyal imperial soldiers he fought and killed.”

“Yes they did. It's been over thirty years since the rebellion and it is our hope we can all come to see it for the mistake it was and heal the wounds it caused.”

The judge fell silent as if considering the attorney's words, and Ninal dared hope they might actually have a chance.

“Your Honor, I know my father was loyal to the empire and wanted nothing more than to be a part of creating the future envisioned by the emperor. It broke his heart to fight his colleagues in the military and he never would have done so if he saw another way,” she spoke up.

“I find it hard to believe you were old enough to remember much about him.”

“I remember how often he was gone, and that every time I saw him he spoke about fighting the monsters that threatened to destroy us all. I've also read everything he ever wrote that I could find and listened to the stories my mother told. I know what kind of man he was.”

“I see,” Nezin said as he leaned back in his chair to study the supplicants before him.

Ninal stole a glance at her husband who gave her an encouraging smile, then looked at their attorney but only received a blank expression from him.

“I believe what you are saying to be true, but unfortunately a man's feelings towards his actions do not change those actions nor erase their consequences. Riken Tenoch participated in an attempt to subvert the emperor's rule on this planet. He was a traitor, and will always be remembered as such,” the judge decreed.

He leaned back over his desk, signed the veto section on the petition displayed on its screen, then sent it off to be filed.

“Your Honor, I respectively ask that you reconsider. Whatever happened in the past, granting forgiveness now would go a long way towards healing old wounds and making our two peoples one again,” the lawyer requested.

“My decision is final. I'm also drafting an order preventing you from appealing it to the courts on Ordeos. You're dismissed,” Nezin responded without looking up.

Husband and wife glanced at each other, then at their lawyer, mutually concluded that was the end of it, then got up and left.

The lawyer went his own way without saying another word upon exiting the office, leaving the couple to find their own way out of the building.

“As I said, one way or the other,” Cyvin remarked under his breath as they walked through the vaulted hallways.

“It seems there is only one way left to us,” Ninal mused.

Wednesday, June 11th, 2313
10:12 P.M.

A man and woman darted across the dark alley, pressed themselves against the back of the building on the other side, and held their breath as they listened for the sounds of pursuit. When they heard nothing, the man leaned out to take a look, then slid back and nodded to his wife, indicating it was clear.

They slowly walked across the lot to the small building on the other side where no lights could be seen, staying alert for soldiers out enforcing the planetary curfew which began two hours ago.

"Who is that?" a voice whispered from the dark doorway when they drew close.

"Cyvin and Ninal Guavanic," the man whispered back.

A door opened with a soft creak, revealing more darkness within, and the two stepped through and closed it behind them before opening the next door into a dimly lit room. The room was so packed with chairs there was little space left around the edges to walk, and every chair was occupied. At the front was a large crate upon which stood a man carefully speaking at a normal volume despite the anger evident in his words.

"All of the major companies are Ordonian owned, leaving us with little opportunity to build something for ourselves unless we work for them. My son works for one of them, and he was recently forced to go offworld or lose his job and be barred from working for any of them ever again. And as long as he is offworld, we are forbidden any form of communication. I couldn't even send him something in the mail the other day."

The new arrivals went to stand by the wall on the right to wait for him to finish talking, but he spotted them before they got there.

"I never expected to see the two of you again."

"We...*I* have had to take a long, hard look at my perspective," Ninal responded.

"Please come up here and tell us what you have learned," Sanjic told her, then stepped off the crate and gestured towards it. Cyvin went up to the front with her and she climbed on the crate where she took a deep breath as she looked at the expectant faces before her.

"When I was younger, I was filled with nothing but hate for the Ordonians, and I wanted nothing more than to destroy them and everything they stand for. This movement was just beginning to form then, and I joined without hesitation, but then I found the journal my father wrote while fighting in the rebellion and I began second guessing my decision. It was clear to me that he didn't want it, that all he wanted was reconciliation with Ordeos, and I feared I was betraying his memory by participating in the preparations for another uprising. Most of you know what happened then," she began, glancing at Sanjic at the last part. His anger regarding their arguments and subsequent parting of ways was apparent, but he was listening.

Then she glanced at her husband who gave her an encouraging smile, and finally she looked back at the crowd.

"I thought we could find a peaceful way to regain our rights as imperial citizens and have done all I could to achieve that these last few years, but all I managed to do was find out how wrong I was. My petition to restore my father's name has been denied by every authority on Nosin without possibility of appeal to Ordeos. Our attorney has abandoned us, and everyone else we have contacted, both Nosine and Ordonian, has refused to take our case. It is clear to me now there is only one way for our rights to be restored, and that is if we take them by force."

That being all she had to say, Ninal stepped down and went to stand by the wall with her husband. Hushed whispers spread through the crowd while Sanjic continued to stare at them, his thoughts hidden behind a stern expression.

Total silence fell when Sanjic finally moved to stand next to the crate, but he didn't climb on it this time.

"We hold no governing authority on our planet, our children are sent away with no ability to keep in touch, and our heroes are denied their due while the pleas of their children are ignored. What reason can possibly remain to stop us from seizing back our rights?"

The silence remained as he stared long and hard at the attendees, but a mounting fury rose from them that could be felt as easily as any flame.

"Return home. You will receive instructions soon, and we will once again be the masters of our own destiny," Sanjic concluded, then he walked over to Ninal and Cyvin as a line formed at the door for people to leave one or two at a time.

"We're in this now, and your story was the catalyst, so you'd better be sure you're committed this time," he hissed.

"We are. What do you want us to do?" Ninal responded.

"Your father was already a hero to the cause, so we will use their continued denial of his rightful status to fuel the fire. When it starts, you'll be here in the city to motivate the people and remind them why they're fighting. Cyvin will stay with you to keep you safe."

"Sounds good to me," Cyvin agreed, but Sanjic locked eyes with Ninal until she showed her consent with a nod.

"Be ready to fight on a moment's notice. We'll contact you when we're ready," Sanjic ordered, then stalked off.

Monday, July 7th, 2313
8:17 A.M.

"Remember how many lives depend on your cooperation, including your own," Sanjic commented as the base's main gate came into view.

The Ordonian driver took a deep breath and nodded to show his understanding.

They pulled up to the guardhouse where the driver's identification was confirmed by retinal scan before he handed over a tablet showing his orders along with the convoy's cargo manifest.

"You're late," the guard observed, and Sanjic gripped the pistol hidden under his arm a little tighter.

"There was a wreck in the road. We comlinked ahead with a report," the driver responded.

"Are you aware of the current program to eliminate all such inefficiency, starting with the military then continuing on to everyone else?"

"Yes, sir, but we couldn't continue until the road was cleared."

"You should have prepared for such delays before you even set out."

"I understand, sir."

"I'm placing a warning in your record. Now, explain why there is a Nosine in your vehicle," the guard demanded as he gave Sanjic a pointed look.

"He's part of a new program integrating them into military operations working loading docks, construction sites, or anywhere else their strength can be put to use. Why should civilian companies be the only ones to benefit?"

"I haven't heard anything about this, but I do know regulations forbid allowing Nosines anywhere near military centers."

"Those regulations are under review, or at least that's what I was told. I don't know why you weren't informed," the driver insisted. The guard stared at him, then looked at Sanjic again who glared back without offering any explanations of his own.

"Very well. Move on," he finally relented, stepping away from the truck and swiping a finger towards the gate to signal someone to open it.

"Take us to the command center," Sanjic ordered once they were through.

"Where are they going?" the driver questioned upon seeing in his mirrors the other three trucks turn onto other roads.

"Just do as you're told."

Some rustling in the back indicated his fellow rebels were preparing to strike, but the cab was silent as they proceeded towards the center of the base.

When they turned west, Sanjic raised his eyes towards the horizon and imagined the capital in the distance where the pressure from decades of oppression was nearing its inevitable climax.

Dovlik City
8:28 A.M.

"We are here to see the governor," Ninal announced to the gate guard with Cyvin and another man standing on either side of her.

"The governor does not meet with Nosines," the man responded without even looking at any of them.

"It's about my father, a man who fought for the empire during the Alien Wars. He deserves recognition for that, but the courts refuse to do anything about it."

"That is not the governor's concern."

"We're making it his concern," Cyvin threatened, then grabbed the guard and threw him to the ground while simultaneously disarming him. The other man with them did the same with the guard on the opposite side of the gate while Ninal rushed into the gatehouse, knocked out the operator with a punch to the jaw, then opened the gate.

More guards rushed towards them from the compound interior, but twice as many Nosines rushed out from the surrounding streets and buildings to meet them.

The guards began shooting and the attackers followed suit, quickly dispatching the Ordonians with superior numbers. Alarms sounded, and metal barriers slid down over all the doors and windows on the government offices, but the defenders soon discovered this was no mere rabble when the Nosines blew open the doors with explosives and stormed inside.

When it was clear, Ninal and her husband entered the building and made their way to the governor's office on the top floor, encountering no opposition. Upon arriving in the office they were greeted with the sight of the governor kneeling on the floor with hands behind his head while three Nosines stood guard.

They ignored him and went straight to his desk where Ninal sat in his chair as Cyvin activated the public address system.

"I am Ninal Guavanic, daughter of Riken Tenoch, a hero of the Alien Wars who died fighting for the rights of his people. Thirty years later, those rights are still denied us and we are offered no hope for their restoration."

She paused, looked at her husband who smiled and nodded in encouragement, then she took a deep breath and continued.

"This can be tolerated no longer. I call upon all Nosines to rise up and take back those rights and declare we will not allow anyone to treat us as second-class citizens. The fight has already begun, and many around this planet are seizing control of Ordonian government offices and military installations. Join us, and together we will secure our freedom now and forever," she finished.

"This will never work. We defeated you once, and will do so again, and this time you will be left with nothing at all," the governor spoke up.

"Last time we were forced to act before we could prepare, but this time we are ready to face anything you can throw at us. We *will* be free."

Ordeos
Ordeos Prime
9:51 A.M.

"The local garrison is unable to turn this around?" Emperor Razis Lentaise questioned after studying the tactical situation on Nosin.

"They are requesting reinforcements, Majesty. Nearly half of our bases are under rebel control, the rest are under heavy attack, and the cities are swarming with rioters," Primary Mason, his top military commander, responded.

"Orbital control remains secure?"

"Affirmative."

"Evacuate all our people, military and otherwise, from Dovlik City. Send all available units in the system to secure our bases, and prepare for a nuclear strike on the capital," Lentaise ordered.

"Nuclear, sir? Are you sure you want to do that?"

"These people clearly have not learned from their previous mistake, but this time we will leave no doubt regarding the cost of disloyalty. Destroy the city."

The primary responded by snapping his right fist to his heart in the imperial salute then moved off to enact the emperor's orders.

"Master Knight Kazlin," Lentaise said, and a man in a grey and red uniform stepped up beside him.

"When this is over, we will establish total control on the Nosine population. Their only purpose will be to serve the empire and every aspect of their lives will be determined by us. Prepare to implement this policy."

The Nosine people had proven themselves a troublesome sort, but he would see to it they would never again be a problem.

Nosin
Tiansen Base
5:07 P.M.

"Regroup at the command center!" Sanjic shouted, struggling to be heard above the gunfire and explosions. "Fall back!"

They'd almost had the base under their control in the morning, but then scores of Ordonians had returned from the capital and counterattacked with nearly overwhelming force. He couldn't understand why they weren't more concerned with restoring order in the city, but didn't have time to worry about it.

"Commander! Dovlik City is ours!" his lieutenant reported.

"That doesn't help us much if we can't secure this base! Call for reinforcements! We'll hole up at the command center until they get here!"

He suddenly realized that he wasn't having to shout as loud and looked around to see that they were no longer taking any fire.

"Cease fire!" he called out, and an eerie silence fell as the rebels stopped shooting.

"What's going on?" the lieutenant whispered, but Sanjic only shushed him.

A bright flash illuminated the area, causing them all to instinctively duck and cover their eyes. It dissipated a moment later, and Sanjic looked towards the west to see a fiery mushroom cloud growing where Dovlik City used to be.

He slowly stood, dropping his rifle in amazement as those around him did the same.

Ninal, Cyvin, hundreds of rebels, and over a million other people – dead. Vaporized in an instant, murdered by people they once thought their saviors.

Dozens of imperial troops surrounded them, but they didn't react. There was nothing left to do.

All was lost.

Change, Survival, and Vendettas

Palcion
Sunday, March 7th, 2343
12:12 A.M.

"What do you want, Snake?" Captain Bloodsworn demanded to know of his rival.

There were over a dozen pirate ships roaming the stars, but Snake and his crew were one of the only two which he considered a credible threat. It was that respect which had prompted him to agree to meet in this festering swamp where he had to wear an ultrasonic transmitter just to keep from being eaten alive.

"If I wanted to hurt you, these guys wouldn't be able to stop me," Captain Snake observed as he gestured towards the four large men standing on either side of his counterpart, each one inches away from sticking a foot in the muck which surrounded them. Neither side had brought any light with them, but Bloodsworn could still see a devious smile within the pale face of the other captain.

"Maybe, but it makes me feel better making it as hard for you as possible," Bloodsworn shot back, careful to keep his own tanned face from betraying any emotion. Only one pirate accompanied Snake, but he knew better than to let his guard down around this smallish man whose smile only grew wider at his remark.

"The times in which we find ourselves offer many opportunities for those capable enough to see and understand them. I have learned of one such opportunity, but I require more resources."

"You're proposing we work together on a raid?"

"Precisely."

"What's the target?"

"With the alien wars over, the Vehlan Union is ending its isolationism and is looking to grab some of the unclaimed territories for itself. They established a prospecting outpost in a system not far from here, and word is they have already collected quite a few minerals and jewels," Snake explained.

"It's a bad idea to make an enemy of the union. Since they didn't participate in the exterminations, they didn't suffer any of the setbacks the other nations did. They can and will come after us."

"Without the aliens to distract them, it is only a matter of time before the Ordonians and others decide to hunt us down. They are regrouping now, but that won't last forever. If we are to survive, we must become big enough to outlast them."

"We survive by knowing our limits. The Vehlans are too strong," Bloodsworn balked.

"Yes, they are strong, but also limited. Their isolation kept them safe, but left them with little to no logistical support when it comes to working outside their own borders. We can easily stay ahead of anything they send after us."

This was something Bloodsworn had not considered, and learning it now was enough to get him to pause and consider the alliance.

He had done well with just his one ship during the chaos of constant war, but now that they were headed into a time of peace he had become aware of how vulnerable he really was. If he had enough money to hire other ships, or even to establish a permanent base, then his future would be a lot more secure.

"Tell me all the details," he finally relented.

Grilke
Thursday, March 11th, 2343
8:35 A.M.

"When was the last time you were planetside?" the dark-skinned Vehlan lieutenant remarked as he took Snake's fake id card and inserted it into a portable reader.

"A couple days ago, why?" Snake responded, knowing full well the question was due to his pale skin.

"Just curious," the kid quickly covered as he handed back the card and waved the disguised pirate captain through the checkpoint.

The soldier quickly finished with the other nine members of the group, all of them dressed as miners, then told them they could continue on and check in with their new supervisor.

They walked away from the landing pad towards the largest of the six buildings with bags slung over shoulders while the captain gave some last minute instructions without slowing his pace.

"You have your assignments. Cut off their communications, disable security systems, and stake out the vault. Go."

He finished talking just as they entered the office building, and the group behind him broke into three groups of three and headed in different directions, but he continued alone deeper into the building.

"Good morning, Genkins," he said as he stepped through the door marked Mining Supervisor.

"Captain Snake! I...I...I wasn't expecting you to come yourself," the broad-shouldered man sitting behind the desk at the opposite wall reacted. His dark hair was spotted with gray and his skin appeared as leather, but the blue eyes that beheld his visitor were filled with a terror that contradicted his rugged appearance.

"There are times I must handle matters personally, and this is one of those times," Snake explained as he closed the door behind him.

"I've done everything you asked."

"Yes, which is why I feel you have earned this," the captain revealed as he approached the desk while holding up a data chip.

"The videos?"

"Every last one."

"I won't have to do anything else?"

"Nothing at all," Snake said with a smile, then dropped the chip on the desk and headed for the door, but stopped without opening it and said, "You could come with us. No more rules and expectations to be broken then used against you."

"No. I'm done with this. I just want to go back to a normal life," Genkins responded firmly.

"That's unfortunate. If I could blackmail you into betraying your employers and nation, then someone else could do it again to get you to betray me."

In an instant, Snake turned and shot the man in the chest.

"You might have still been useful, if you had only had the good sense to accept my offer," he commented, then returned the pistol to its concealed holster and left.

Gunship Fury
8:57 A.M.

The clock displayed on the main screen inched towards the agreed upon time for the coordinated strike as Captain Bloodsworn stared at it from the command chair, chin resting on left fist supported by the elbow propped on the armrest.

“I hope you know what you’re doing, Captain,” Barz, his second in command, commented from his right.

“Either we risk a quick death here, or guarantee a slow death scrounging for scraps where governments won’t chase us,” Bloodsworn declared.

“I’m as determined to find riches as you are, but Snake is not a man to be trusted.”

“He can be trusted as long as he needs us.”

“But once he has the haul, what guarantee do we have that he’ll give us our share?”

“He may need us again in the future. If we do our part, he will want to remain on our good side,” Bloodsworn insisted, finally silencing Barz and his doubts.

It was time. The captain nodded to Barz, who then gave the order to jump into normal space.

The clock disappeared to be replaced by the image of a Vehlan cruiser above a lumpy, brown and gray planet, then a series of three missiles, their engines glowing blue, shot out from the Fury. Two struck the cruiser forward center while the last one hit it on the starboard side.

“Enemy comms and hangar disabled.”

“Target the weapons next,” Bloodsworn commanded as the enemy ship swung towards them. It fired a missile of its own, but the gunship’s interceptors shot it down before it even got close.

The pirates attempted to fly over the cruiser, but its captain anticipated this and pivoted up as he was turning, thus bringing his main guns to bear.

“Stay behind them!” Bloodsworn demanded as two direct hits rocked the ship.

“I’m trying!” Helm shouted back as he course corrected.

Both ships buffeted each other with their point defense guns as they passed, doing little damage except to weaken the armor.

They turned back towards each other, and this time the smaller gunship proved quicker and lined up a shot with its main gun first. The railgun round destroyed the cruiser's port cannon, then the pirates accelerated away just in time to cause the return shot to pass beneath them.

"Good thing that planet's mostly uninhabited," Barz joked when he saw the missed shot heading for the planet, but Bloodsworn ignored him and ordered Helm to bring them around again.

They didn't get a clear shot at the weapons this time, but the captain ordered Tactical to fire anyway.

The shot struck the cruiser's side precisely where the turrets had torn into it moments earlier, and the impact blew a large hole that exposed the interior of the ship causing debris and bodies to fly out into space.

Hurt, but not crippled, the Vehlans fired a salvo of four missiles. Three were destroyed en route, but the fourth scored a hit near the thrusters, disabling one of them.

"This is Captain Snake to Fury. Haul is secured and we're on our way up."

"About time," Barz muttered.

"Give me manual control of the missiles," Captain Bloodsworn ordered as he swung a console over his lap, which he then used to fire another trio of missiles.

Instead of locking on to the enemy ship, he controlled their flight himself and kept them spinning in erratic circles as they traversed the empty space between the combatants. The Vehlans still managed to shoot two of them down, but the third got through and overshot the cruiser, but then he reversed it and sent it into their thrusters.

The resulting explosion destroyed their main propulsion, even sending one thruster spinning away from the ship, then another railgun shot destroyed their missile launcher. Their remaining weapons were now useless without the ability to maneuver.

"Stand down," Bloodsworn told his crew, then pushed the console aside to stand up and stretch.

A lone shuttle appeared on their screens then, and when it sent the confirmation signal, he gave the order to follow it back into hyperspace.

Fury
Tuesday, March 16th, 2343
2:02 P.M.

"Our business is concluded, Snake. What do you want now?" Bloodsworn snapped when his nemesis' pale face appeared on the main screen.

Then he noticed the other captain's somber look, and his frustration immediately turned to grave concern. What could have possibly happened to grieve an experienced, and pragmatic, pirate such as Snake?

"I thought you would want to know that shortly after we left Grilke, Captain Blackheart attacked and stole what we were unable to carry. He completely destroyed the other cruiser protecting the system, then finished off the one you disabled before landing and killing every last person at the outpost," Snake relayed without any hint of the mischievous smile which accompanied most of his remarks.

"There were families there preparing to start a colony. With children."

"All dead. He was there a lot longer than he needed to be, so I must assume those deaths weren't quick."

Silence thick enough to cut descended on the bridge as everyone present stared at the screen. They were all criminals by trade who wouldn't hesitate to kill to achieve their ends, but even they couldn't fathom why someone would do such a thing. There was nothing to be gained from slaughtering those people.

"This cannot go unanswered," Bloodsworn finally decreed.

"I agree," Snake responded simply, although Bloodsworn wondered if the other captain was more concerned about how the resulting reputation for all pirates would be bad for business than he was for the morality of the situation.

He thanked his rival for the information, then had the channel cut.

"Barz."

"Yes, Captain?"

"Make it known that I will pay a bounty to anyone, pirate or not, who brings me proof they have killed a member of Blackheart's crew. The assassin will receive the equivalent of one-thousand Ordonian destins for a crew member, five-thousand for an officer, and one-hundred thousand for Blackheart himself."

"Are you sure you want to do that? I don't like what he did any more than you do, but going to war with another pirate won't do either side any good."

"I'm sure. From this day forward, Blackheart is my mortal enemy."

Excised History

Eritania
Tuesday, January 17th, 2417
3:03 A.M.

The frigid temperatures of deep winter went unnoticed by the tall, wiry man as he crept through the trees, not even his full-body armor causing him to make a single noise.

His helmet's nightvision revealed a cliff before him, and he approached the edge where he squatted down and peered at the massive building in the valley below as the others gathered around him. Not fortunate enough to be supplied with the new armor, they wore special masks under their goggles to prevent their breath from fogging the air and risk giving away their position.

The first man zoomed his optics in on the old factory and slowly scanned every inch of it. Nearly all of the windows were cracked, broken, or missing their glass entirely, and none of them revealed any light or movement.

After the other teams reported the same findings, he used hand-signals to order his sniper to provide overwatch from the cliff, then with one word over comms ordered all teams to move in.

There was no doubt their targets were inside, and he found himself wishing they could just bomb the place and be done with it, but if the task were that easy they wouldn't have sent a Star Knight. This was foreign soil, making an overt attack out of the question, and they had to personally verify that every last person and item was destroyed.

He would have also preferred if only knights were assigned to the mission, but as it was they had to rely on military special forces with only the team leaders being knights. The order didn't have the numbers for an operation such as this, and technically they weren't supposed to conduct missions of this nature anyway.

They finally reached the factory, and after a short pause to confirm they were still alone, the knight led his team through an open bay door and in a quick sweep of the room beyond, but all they found was some old machinery.

Each team reported their entry positions clear, so he mandated two soldiers from each one maintain position while the remainder continued forward.

"Knight Ensias to Knight Captain Grence. Have located entrance to sub-levels. Evidence of recent activity. Please advise," the whispered report came over the comms.

"Proceed. En route to support. All others, continue search."

The captain checked Ensias' position on a small map which displayed itself on his goggles, then headed for the northeast wall.

He found the stairs with the door swung wide open and a soldier standing guard opposite it, then headed down with his teammates following two at a time.

They came out on a long, concrete corridor with pipes on the walls and ceiling, halfway down of which he could see the other team.

He was about to contact them when a blazing light suddenly overwhelmed the nightvision.

"Ah!" he shouted in unison with his men as he backed into the wall and instinctively covered his eyes. The optics deactivated automatically, but as soon as they did the light disappeared to leave them just as blind in the dark.

The enhancement activated again, but then so did the light.

"Turn them off and leave them off!" he shouted to the others as he fumbled to find the switch on the side of his own helmet.

The strobe effect continued as he willed his eyes to adjust faster before someone started shooting, but then he finally saw the fixture on the ceiling and shot it.

"No. Flashlights only," Grence ordered when he saw a soldier about to reactivate his nightvision. Stealth was clearly no longer an option, and there could be more light traps.

Upon activating the light on his rifle, the knight shone it down the corridor, but didn't see anything, not even the other team.

"All teams, watch for traps. We triggered one down here, so assume the targets know we are here. Ensias, report."

No answer.

He tried again, but met with the same result.

"Rollins, Cuni, take point. Move out."

The team moved forward again while sweeping their lights over every surface.

The only sounds were their slow footsteps and steady breathing as they inched their way forward.

Then Rollins pitched forward and would have fallen if not for Grence grabbing him and pulling him back. He then joined the two on point and all three of them pointed their lights into the ten meter deep pit to reveal a sight that brought Grence's blood to a boil.

All seven of those that had entered the underground ahead of them lay at the bottom, impaled on spikes faintly lit by energy fields which must have made it possible for them to penetrate the armor.

"Guards, remain at your posts. Everyone else, converge on my position."

"Sir!" Cuni shouted and pointed, and Grence looked up in time to see someone duck through a door to the right on the other side of the pit.

"After him!"

"How?"

The pit was too large to jump over, so Grence looked around for anything to make a bridge and spotted the pipes over their heads. He shot them on either side of the gap and they fell on top of it where Rollins and Cuni quickly pushed them up next to each other and held them in place while the others ran across.

The door led to another corridor similar to the first, and the knight captain ran down it with zero regard for more traps. If his quarry was safe, then so was he.

"Stop!"

Whoever it was responded by turning around long enough to fire a shot, but he missed and opted to flee again.

The knight almost had him when he suddenly darted to the left, causing him to overshoot and have to skid to a halt before swinging back.

He finally chased the man through a door to emerge in a room lit by an orange glow where he found himself facing three men and one woman with pistols aimed at him, the man on the right panting heavily. He was also the only one fully dressed while the others had nothing on but shirts and shorts.

"Drop the gun!" the man with thinning gray hair in the middle demanded, but Grence raised his rifle to point at them.

"Where is Sleise?" he questioned, his voice steady.

"We will shoot!"

His team caught up with him then and spread out on either side of him with rifles at the ready.

"Where is Sleise?" the captain repeated.

Four pairs of eyes danced over the six armored men standing before them, then the younger criminals looked at their elder whose face had hardened with resolve.

"For truth!" he declared and opened fire, but the slugs of the antiquated railguns bounced harmlessly off the soldiers who then rushed forward and disarmed them in deference to Grence's standing orders to take them alive.

The four of them were cuffed and made to kneel before the knight captain just as the remaining teams showed up. He ordered the soldiers to stand guard outside while the knights searched through the contraband which he could now see spread out on several tables to his left.

"Where is Arcon Sleise?"

His only answer was defiant stares.

"You should take into consideration the fact we are Star Knights of the Ordeon Empire, and as knights we are authorized to use any means necessary in defense of the emperor and his decrees."

This news did not affect the older man, but the eyes of his companions grew wide with unmistakable fear.

"Is he here?"

"No," the dark-haired man answered, still out of breath from the run.

"It's all here, Knight Captain. The last evidence of any sapient life other than our own," a knight reported.

"The book?"

"Missing."

"You're too late. Arcon finished it and is taking it to the people," the older man taunted with a smile.

"We will deal with him eventually. Until then, no one will take him seriously without any hard evidence to back up his claims," Grence responded, then nodded at the knights who proceeded to throw everything into a pile on the floor.

He watched the captives as they stared at the scene with horror. When they were finished, a knight poured an accelerant on it then backed away to make room for another one to shoot it, igniting it with the laser shot.

The horror of the prisoners slowly gave way to defeat as they watched all they had worked so hard to gather go up in flames, then they finally looked away when four of the knights stood before them and aimed at their heads.

"Fire."

Vehla
United
Thursday, January 19th, 2417
2:00 P.M.

"I appreciate you agreeing to meet with me, Chancellor," Arcon Sleise greeted upon entering the office of the union's highest political leader. He approached the burly, middle-aged man seated behind the desk, but his outstretched hand was ignored.

"As opposed to having you arrested, you mean?" Chancellor Fenik responded.

"What do you mean?" Arcon asked as he dropped the hand and looked side-to-side, but the action only confirmed that they were alone.

"Did you really think that an assumed name would fool my security team?"

"I couldn't think of any other way," he admitted. His first instinct was to give everything up for lost, but his spirits lifted when he realized he wouldn't have gotten this far unless the chancellor was interested in hearing what he had to say.

"Then this means you have finished, but lack a means of distribution."

Arcon pulled a thick binder from the bag dangling from his right hand and placed it on the desk.

"Since Vehla wasn't involved, you're the only ones who would be willing to get the word out," he explained.

The chancellor glared at the book a moment, then promptly stood up and went to the table to the right of his desk where he prepared himself a drink.

"There are good reasons for people not to know," he claimed after taking a sip, his tone softer than before.

"This is our past! Our real past! People deserve to know the truth!" Arcon retorted. He trembled as he prepared to rebut any argument to the contrary, but then Fenik looked at him, his eyes heavy with sadness and fatigue, and the fight just went out of him.

"Do you really think people need to know that humans are a race of mass murderers who wiped out over a dozen alien civilizations, most of whom never did us any harm?"

Arcon was silent for a moment. This wasn't anything he hadn't heard before, but the way Fenik said it somehow made him feel as though he were being selfish for wanting to reveal the truth.

"It's what happened. What good does it do anyone to cover it up?"

The chancellor returned to his seat, and finally offered Arcon a seat by gesturing to a chair in front of the desk, but he just shook his head no.

"Rage is a powerful and often uncontrollable emotion as was proved by the exterminations. Guilt can be just as bad. Not everyone can handle the truth, and I have no doubt society would break down as a result. We would destroy ourselves without help from any aliens."

"If you are so sure about that, then why am I here?"

"Because you are right about one thing, which is that this history cannot be allowed to be forgotten entirely."

"That much I can accomplish without your help."

"An abandoned factory on Eritania was found burned to the ground yesterday morning. Four corpses were discovered in a gutted sub-level. That wouldn't happen to affect your plans, would it?" Fenik challenged, and Arcon finally sank into the chair as he stared at him in disbelief.

"You killed them?"

"No, it was the Ordonians."

"And you're going to let them get away with trespassing in union territory and murdering union citizens?"

"We can't go to war without revealing the reasons for it, but our knowledge of the incursion does give us certain leverage over the empire."

Grief and anger rose in Arcon, but he forced it down by swallowing and nodded for Fenik to continue. He was completely powerless here.

"I want to publish this book and give at least two copies to the leaders of each nation, including the Ordeon Empire. That way the truth will be remembered without endangering the public good."

"The Ordonians will never go for it. They want it forgotten. They are the ones who led the exterminations after all," Arcon disputed.

"I have already spoken to many of the other national leaders, and they want this. If the empire refuses to accept it, they are willing to form a coalition to force the issue. The attack on your friends gives us a public reason for such an action, given the alteration of certain facts."

"What about me?"

"You will be granted your freedom in exchange for your future silence. You've spent twenty years on this crusade, and have managed to complete your task against all odds. It's time to go home, and you can do so knowing you did everything in your power to right a wrong," Fenik offered.

He still thought people should know the truth, but Arcon had to admit the man was right. There was no more evidence to be had, all his friends were dead, and there was nothing he could do about any of it.

The outcome wasn't what he wanted, but his task was done, so he stood up and nodded at the book as he looked the chancellor in the eyes.

"Keep it," was all he said, then he was out the door.

Part II
Character Stories

Heart of a Leader

Persidia
Tuesday, October 2nd, 2694
4:31 P.M.

The artillery shot screeched over Leon and exploded on the beach several meters behind him, raining down blackened sand as he buried his face in the mud under the deployable elastic barrier, his feet and lower legs partly submerged in the muck behind him.

When he looked up again, he saw a burning palm tree waving against a bright blue sky marred by streaks of dark smoke.

"There's too many of them, Captain!" a soldier cried out.

"We will hold!" Leon shouted back.

It didn't matter that they'd already lost their base and all they had left were these hastily dug foxholes leading toward the beach. He was not about to let another planet fall to the enemy.

The artillery barrage ended and was immediately replaced by constant laser fire pelting the barrier, but the shots did not penetrate. At least these Imps hadn't received their new plasma guns yet.

"Return fire!"

Dozens of Vehlan soldiers in trenches and dugouts popped into firing positions and opened up with everything they had, including the captain.

The first line of advancing Ordonians fell to the opening volley or quickly backpedaled, but the next line dove into cover amid the leafy plants, their adaptive camouflage quickly making them all but invisible. This afforded them the breathing room to take careful aim at the defenders and begin picking them off.

It wasn't long before the defending fire began to falter, and the Ordonians took advantage of it by running out and dragging their wounded comrades back to relative safety. One ran into Leon's field of view, but he quickly downed him with two shots to the torso.

The soldier on Leon's right suddenly fell back to land with a splash in the mud, so he set down his rifle and crawled over to him only to find a smoking hole in the center of his face where his nose used to be.

"We have to get out of here!"

"No!" Leon shouted as he retrieved his rifle and returned to the firing line, but he only got off a few shots before the battery ran out.

He didn't have a replacement, so he threw it to the side and grabbed the one dropped by the dead soldier, but upon checking its charge he learned it only had a few shots left as well.

He looked around at the rest of his soldiers and saw many of them had stopped firing and were frantically looking around.

"For the union!" he shouted as he popped up again and opened fire, taking out a few enemy soldiers who had dared attempting to advance.

They were not going to lose again. Not while they had any fight left in them.

An Ordonian with a plasma streamer strapped to his back charged into the open towards Leon's position. He tried to shoot him, but again his weapon clicked with an empty charge. The soldier skidded to a halt, planted his feet in the dirt, then let loose with a stream of burning white plasma and Leon was forced to duck again to avoid having his face scorched off.

Thick sludge oozed on to the ground as the barrier began to melt, requiring the defenders to keep their unprotected faces away from it, but even their armor did little to protect them so Leon waved them back into the mud to buy some time.

"We have to retreat!"

"No! We've retreated too much already!"

"We have nothing left to fight with!"

"We'll fight hand-to-hand if we have to!"

"This is pointless!" the malcontent asserted as he threw his rifle away.

The captain was about to order him to pick it up, but was interrupted by a broadcast from command.

"All units retreat. We are abandoning the planet. Repeat. We are abandoning the planet. Retreat to your transports."

The soldier arguing with Leon gave him a look that said, "Can we go now?", and he was forced to confirm the order through gritted teeth.

They ran towards the beach where escape transports waited under sand colored tarps. The captain pulled a detonator from a pouch on his belt, then activated it when they were far enough away. Several explosions ripped apart their fortifications, but he did not look back to see how well it worked.

Troop Transport
6:47 P.M.

The space battle still raging around the planet was clearly visible through the window on the opposite side of the passenger bay from Leon, but it was the rapidly receding planet that held his gaze. It's massive ocean dotted with islands around a single continent covered in mountains and valleys was once a warm, inviting sight for any Vehlan, but now the smoke streaked skies only served to remind him of all they had lost.

No matter how hard they fought, they just couldn't seem to stop this latest Ordonian incursion into their territory. Now, five years after breaching the border, the invaders were poised to take Redlode, the union's primary source of fuel. If that fell, the war might as well be over and the decades of sacrifice would be wasted.

There was a flash, and the view outside was replaced with the off-white colors of hyperspace.

"We had to get out of there. There was nothing we could do," the soldier on Leon's left assured him.

The hopelessness in the man's voice seemed to shake something loose inside him, and he clenched his jaw in determination.

The first stop for the retreating soldiers would be a staging base on Qaldova, a moon orbiting the outermost gas giant in the Redlode system. His sister was serving with the medical corps there, and a dose of her stubborn optimism was exactly what he needed right now.

Then it would be on to Vehla where he could find the leaders of this war and insist they do better. If he had to take matters into his own hands to win this war for his people, then that's exactly what he would do.

Vehla
Friday, October 5th, 2694
10:04 A.M.

"Thank you for seeing me, Major," Captain Tyquese greeted his superior upon entering his office.

"We both have a lot of work to do. What is so important?" Major Vuie asked without looking up from his desk's digital display.

"I have developed a strategy for your review, sir. A way to repel the Ordonian invasion."

That got the major to look up.

"You don't trust your superiors to figure something out?" he growled.

"This isn't about trust, sir. It's about doing my part to win this war and protect our people," Tyquese insisted.

The major narrowed his eyes as he glared at his subordinate, but the captain did not flinch as he stared back with all the respect he could muster.

Eventually Vuie looked back at his desk, cleared a space in the center, then waved a hand at it as he leaned back. Tyquese activated the holographic display on his palco, the microcomputer embedded in his left palm, found the desk on the network and sent over the file containing his plan which automatically opened to reveal a map of the Vehlan territories.

"Our defense has focused on stopping their frontal advance but we're unable to field the necessary resources without compromising our defenses elsewhere. I've studied the empire's deployments and have discovered that they've left their flanks weak so as to use overwhelming force at the front. I believe a coordinated counterattack against each flank can break through then use hit-and-run attacks to disrupt their supply lines and slowly starve them out," the captain explained.

"That would leave us vulnerable," the major objected, but he was studying the map with its proposed resource deployments carefully, his dark brow furrowed in thought.

"Once the counterattack begins, we won't need as much at the front."

"It's risky. We should put everything we have into defending Redlode."

"I understand the importance of defending the Redlode system, sir. It's our main source of fuel for our ships and the last step before Vehla itself, but with all due respect, we've been attempting a strong defense from the start and it hasn't worked yet. A risk such as this might very well be the last chance we have to stop the enemy," Tyquese pressed.

The major didn't respond but kept looking over the map, occasionally zooming in on a section or moving something around.

Finally, he sighed, stood, and came around the desk with his hand outstretched.

"You might be right. I can't promise it'll be accepted, but I'll forward your proposal up the chain of command."

"Thank you, sir," Tyquese said as he shook the man's hand.

When he left the office, he did so with a fresh hope rising within him that threatened to put a smile on his face. They might not use the strategy, and it might not work even if they did, but at least he knew he was doing everything he could to put an end to this threat to his people.

Vehla

United

Wednesday, October 15th, 2694

9:49 A.M.

"Just two weeks of training and they've already shipped my little brother off to Redlode," Leon heard someone say as he stepped out of the car. He looked towards the source to see two women in dark business clothes walking past. There was still time before his meeting in the capitol building looming before him, so he chose to linger and hear more of the conversation.

"I hear that's how it is with all the draftees. They're not doing much more than putting a gun in their hands and telling them which way to point it," the second woman observed.

"The government forces people to fight, then doesn't even give them the means to survive. Where is this freedom they're supposed to be protecting?"

The pair walked out of earshot as Leon sadly watched them go. His own deeply held belief in the union's cause led him to sign up long before the implementation of the draft, but he couldn't fault these two for their feelings. Many of the government's recent actions also had him wondering if they'd already lost that which they were supposed to be stopping the Ordonians from taking.

Once again he reminded himself that much had to be sacrificed in war and that matters would improve following their victory, then held his head high as he marched up the expansive white stone steps into the capitol. At least his own little brother had actually had the sense to enlist in the fleet before getting drafted and was currently assigned to a patrol unit on the border with the Merchant's Interest intercepting pirates.

He turned to the right after entering, got into the first elevator, then took it two floors down to the sub-level containing satellite offices for the military where his major had ordered him to report. One long hallway connected all the rooms, and he walked down it until he found the conference room at the center where he knocked on the door and entered when bidden.

Inside was not only Major Vuie standing at the head of the table as he had expected, but also General Frederick Reno, the commander-in-chief of the entire Vehlan military. He came to attention and snapped his right hand to forehead in salute.

"As you were, Captain," Vuie commanded, so he dropped the salute but remained stiff.

"You are here because I have decided to use your proposed strategy," Reno revealed. On cue, Vuie stepped up to the table and activated its holographic display which showed a revised version of Leon's plan.

"I don't understand. I thought we were moving the bulk of our forces to Redlode," the captain confessed as he looked at the tactical map.

The Redlode system was lit in yellow with green arrows leading to it from all over the union indicating troop and fleet deployments which seemed to confirm what he'd heard, but there were also two blue circles in empty space on either side of the red zone indicating enemy held territory. Blue arrows led to these locations, but there were far fewer of them than the green going towards Redlode.

"That's what we want people to think because that's what we want the Imps to think," Vuie revealed.

"The troops going to Redlode are nothing but draftees rushed through training so we can use them to pad our numbers. We don't expect them to repel an attack. All available veteran volunteers are being used to create a pair of fleets to attack the enemy's flanks as per your suggestion," Reno elaborated.

It was an honor for them to use his strategy, but it looked like they had everything under control and he was beginning to wonder why he was there.

"I don't know if there's anything I can add at this point, sir," he admitted.

"I am placing you in command of the primary fleet," Reno decreed, causing Leon to finally look away from the map and at his superior with mouth agape.

"Me, sir?"

"It's your idea."

"Yes, but I'm an infantry officer."

"You have received fleet training in preparation for promotion, including command training, correct?"

"Yes, sir."

"Then you are capable of leading these men and women in the execution of your own strategy," Reno insisted.

"Yes, sir. I appreciate you placing your confidence in me," Leon agreed, but he felt anything but appreciative. The thought of spending that much time in space, crammed into a ship with thousands of other people and surrounded by vacuum horrified him, but it didn't matter. He would do his duty.

"Take a seat, Captain. We have a lot of preparation remaining before we can begin."

VUS Ristain
Thursday, November 1st, 2694
6:42 A.M.

The whiteness of hyperspace filled the main screen as Captain Tyquese watched from the command chair, his chin resting on tented fingers as he tried not to think about how far he was from solid ground.

The Ordonians had finished securing the Persidia system and were almost ready to advance, but Leon was ready now. His strike squadron was on its way to attack the enemy garrison at Sherinova while their twin headed towards Tadavin.

It was time to turn this war around.

"In position," Navigation reported, and Commander Winley confirmed they were ready to jump.

The captain took a deep breath as he laid his arms on the rests, then nodded for them to proceed.

Within seconds, the oscillating shades of white on the main screen were replaced with endless black surrounding a blue-white gas giant and its many moons.

"Imp cruiser detected. It's heading deeper into the system at high speed," Tactical announced.

"A patrol."

"Send the nearest bomber wing to disable it. Everyone else, maintain course," Leon ordered.

A single wing of Blacksword bombers broke formation and quickly disabled the cruiser, then rejoined the squadron as it passed by the intact but powerless patroller, and soon the gas giant was behind them and a small grey dot was steadily growing before them.

"Composition of enemy forces."

"Two destroyers, one carrier, and twenty cruisers, five of them medium. The carrier is holding position above the planet but the rest are moving to intercept."

"That's it?" Winley questioned.

"They never thought we'd attack from the sides," Leon responded.

The enemy ships and their fighters, minus the carrier and its complement, formed up to create a wall between them and the planet, but the Vehlans continued to speed towards them with seemingly reckless abandon.

"Phase One, go!"

All of the Vehlan fighters and bombers, hundreds of them, shot ahead of the formation along with a dozen corvettes and opened fire. The smaller Ordonian vessels flared out to avoid the worst of it, then descended on the Vehlans as they drew close.

"Phase Two Destroyers, focus all firepower on enemy destroyer at these coordinates. All others, fire on its escorts," Leon ordered as he used the command interface to the right of his chair to mark the target.

The enemy ships in question attempted to evade and fight back, but there was little they could do against so many and they were soon disabled or destroyed.

Their counterparts on the other flank turned to intercept, but they couldn't fire without hitting their own fighters and cruisers in the center, allowing the ships of Phase Two to pass them and proceed towards the planet without further challenge.

"Phase Three, launch but stay with the formation."

Ten small transport craft exited their various mother ships and formed up beside them as the planet loomed large enough to bring the many mountain ranges and cities into view.

Hundreds of enemy fighters launched from the carrier still in orbit and headed for the Vehlans, but Leon sent his remaining corvettes to intercept them and moved his capitol ships into positions covering the transports.

"Phase Three, go."

The transports broke formation and dove towards separate locations on the planet. Any Ordonian fighters that gave chase were shot down and every landing craft made it through.

"Phases One and Two, fall back," Leon ordered, and his ships turned away from the planet in preparation for a jump to hyperspace.

"Are we really going to leave them down there without support?" Winley asked.

"They're Azul Guardians. They can survive for a long time without support, and we'll recapture this system properly before they find themselves in any real trouble."

The rest of the squadron made the jump to hyperspace without any trouble where they reported minimal damage and casualties. The Ordonians did not pursue.

"What's the status at Tadavin?" the captain asked, and Communications reported similar results for them.

It wasn't much, but it was a start.

VUS Ristain
Saturday, December 8th, 2694
1:32 P.M.

One month had seen Leon's guerilla squadrons destroy Ordonian reinforcements intended for Sherinova, Tadavin, and the front along with several supply shipments. So far it had been enough to slow the enemy advance, but the captain was seeing little evidence of it weakening their lines so he was currently sequestered in his ship's tactical center looking for a way to inflict maximum damage.

"Captain!" someone shouted, and he looked towards the main tactical screen to see the Redlode system blinking red. So the Imps had given up on finding him and were proceeding with their advance after all.

"When did it start?"

"Just a few minutes ago, sir."

The captain nodded and returned his attention to the auxiliary screen he was using.

"What are we going to do, sir?"

"Our defenses at Redlode are ready for this, and we're too far away to reinforce them or counterattack behind the enemy lines, but this does present another opportunity for us. Set a rendezvous with the other squadron. Make it as close to the Ordonian border as possible. Set course when ready," Leon responded.

VUS Ristain
Wednesday, December 12th, 2694
3:41 P.M.

Debris floated around Leon's ship, all that remained of the Ordonian fleet meant to reinforce their frontline after their defeat at Redlode. The captain stood in front of the command chair watching it on the main screen, allowing himself to savor the moment for once.

At last they were scoring significant victories against the empire. The tide of war was now turning in their favor, and it was all due to his plan.

It wouldn't be long now before it was the Ordonians who found themselves with enemies on their doorstep.

Persidia
Monday, August 19th, 2695
7:49 P.M.

Night was falling, but one wouldn't know it with all the white plasma bolts, red lasers, and fiery explosions lighting up the island.

The shield flared red on the Lion Tank a few yards to Leon's right, and the captain followed the trajectory of the rocket that struck it and fired several shots at the barrier surrounding the Ordonian base.

He jumped into a blast crater, narrowly avoiding a plasma bolt and coming to rest against the far side next to one of his soldiers.

"We have orbital control! Why don't we just bomb this place to dust?" the man complained.

"Their interceptor cover is too thick. Orbital or aerial bombardments will never get through."

"We could just blockade the planet and starve them out," the woman with them suggested.

"That would cause our own people to suffer as well, and either way we're not going to leave them under Imp subjugation any longer than we have to. Now shut up and do your job!" Leon declared.

A nearby blast threw another soldier into the crater with them followed by a spray of dirt and stones. When it cleared, Leon rolled the soldier onto his back, but he was already dead.

"I'm not going to die here!" the first soldier with Leon shouted. He stood to run away towards the beach, but the captain grabbed his leg and pulled him back down.

"Live free or die trying!" he declared, then ordered everyone to pop smoke.

Within seconds, a curtain of black smoke filled the air between the attacking and defending positions, then Leon ordered the soldiers to cease firing while the tanks laid down suppression fire.

"Now!" he shouted, then vaulted out of the hole and charged the enemy position screaming at the top of his lungs. He stumbled when a plasma bolt grazed his left leg, but quickly compensated and ran faster, using the pain to fuel his anger.

He burst out of the smoke and spotted the barrier coming up quickly with several enemy soldiers behind it taking aim.

Then several lasers came from behind him, knocking down some of the defenders and forcing the rest to duck into cover. He slowed his charge long enough to pull out a grenade and toss it over the low metal wall, then resumed his advance as many of his own troops joined him.

He climbed over the wall, kicked an enemy on the way down, then slammed his rifle into his face, stunning him long enough to disarm him and push aside for the soldier behind him to subdue.

They quickly finished off the defenders in the immediate vicinity, but that left them exposed to those in the trench twenty meters ahead of them. Leon didn't hesitate, but let out another yell and charged once again, this time with his soldiers right at his side, firing as they went.

Some of them fell to the responding defense, but there was no stopping now.

The captain shot a defender, then jumped into the spot he vacated and smashed his rifle butt into the back of the soldier on his left. His rifle was yanked out of his hands from the right, and he ducked just in time to avoid a fist to his face while at the same time drawing his pistol which he used to shoot his attacker in the gut.

He then turned to deal with the first enemy he'd attacked only to discover he was already down and there were Vehlans pressing into the trench, pushing back the defenders.

"Spread out! Secure the trench!" he ordered as he holstered his pistol then reached out for his rifle.

"What about the ones behind us! At the wall!"

"The tanks will keep them busy! Now move!"

There were only a few of them, but they pushed deeper into the enemy position, unleashing on these poor souls the frustration built up over years of losses.

The captain lost himself in the fighting until the point came where there were more Vehlans than Ordonians, so he took a step back and let the others take his place.

It was totally dark now, and when he looked towards the wall he saw it was completely under their control, their tanks parked on the other side firing over their heads. He also noticed that he'd managed to work his way around to the other side of the island and many of the Ordonians were abandoning their positions in favor of the main base which lay on the other side of the anti-air cannons and interceptor guns.

A sharp pain pierced his right side, causing him to place his hand just above his hip as he leaned against the dirt wall. When he brought the hand up he was just able to make out the smear of blood in the dim light. He had gotten stabbed at some point without even realizing it.

As the adrenaline slowly faded away, more pains revealed themselves and he slowly sank to a sitting position as he took stock of the injuries.

His left eye was almost swollen shut, and he could taste blood from a split lip. There was the burn on his leg he'd received during his initial charge, and two more on his right arm, one of them another graze but the other a direct hit which was now throbbing with each heartbeat.

"Captain!" someone shouted as she ran up and knelt before him.

"Report, Lieutenant," he gasped.

"You need medical attention. Medic!"

"I told you to report," he pressed, but she still didn't respond until she'd retrieved a bandage from her kit and pressed it to his stab wound.

"The outer wall is secure and we'll finish with the trenches within minutes. Command has ordered us to hold both positions while our relief pushes forward to take out the cannons at which point they expect the Imps to surrender."

“They’ll try to stop us with a counterattack. We have to be prepared,” Leon observed as he started to get up, but the lieutenant held him down with a hand on his shoulder, then a medic arrived and took over for her.

“The only place you’re going is the medical station, sir. We’ll take care of the Imps,” the lieutenant insisted as she stood up, and he looked up and finally recognized her as the soldier from before who had suggested they simply blockade the planet.

Her face was bruised and dirty, but the fear and doubt from before was gone with nothing but stubborn determination burning in her eyes now. The sight made him smile despite the pain and weariness, and he nodded in acceptance of the situation.

Vehla
Central Command
Monday, March 14th, 2698
10:07 A.M.

A myriad of officers, NCOs, and civilian contractors filled the room with the dull roar of conversation as they continued monitoring the war while guards posted around the room looked on, but Major Leon Tyquese stood quiet and alone in the center staring at the main tactical screen on the far wall. Much work remained, but they’d come a long way in three years and this was as good a time as any to remind himself of what had passed while looking ahead to what was to come.

Promoted for his successful strategy in deterring the Ordonian invasion, he was now a member of General Reno’s personal staff. He still spent most of his time on the front lines, and had only returned to the capital now to assist in planning the next phase.

Only one Vehlan system remained under enemy control, and the liberation fleet was already in position. When that was finished, it would be time to launch their own invasion.

Their people were free once more. It was now his job to ensure they remained that way.

Heart of a Rebel

Swarnlia
Friday, May 17th, 2694
6:07 P.M.

"I won't sit around waiting for someone to destroy everything I care about!" Helen shouted at her father, her face nearly as red as her hair. A couple weeks ago her mother would have found a way to calm everyone down, but without her the argument threatened to spin completely out of control.

"You are eighteen years old, Helen! College is where you belong, not running off to a war!" Reuben yelled back.

"You know nothing about where I belong!"

"I know what's best for you!"

At that, Helen spun around and stomped towards the front door of their house. If any of her brothers and sisters were around, they were staying out of sight. They knew better than to get involved.

"Where do you think you're going?"

"Away from here!"

She yanked open the door and left it open as she marched across the porch, her steps sounding like a battle drum on the old wood.

"Your mother wouldn't approve of this any more than I do!" Reuben declared from the doorway.

She whirled around and pointed an accusing finger towards him.

“Don’t you ever mention her again!” she demanded through clenched teeth, her sight growing blurry as tears stung her eyes.

The middle-aged man before her now looked more weary than angry, and he leaned on the doorframe as he looked at her with the air of someone having to explain a simple concept to an ignorant child.

She hated that look.

“I know the two of you were close, but that doesn’t mean you have to run off and die in a war that is never going to end.”

She clenched her jaw even tighter to hold back the tears now threatening to spill out over her face and looked him right in the eye.

“You don’t understand. You never have, and never will.”

With nothing else to say, she turned and started up the long gravel driveway, and the sound of the door slamming shut quickly followed.

The clothes she was wearing and her stubbornness were all she had now, but it would be enough.

Vehla
Infantry Officer’s Academy
Thursday, October 18th, 2694
9:32 A.M.

“That’s not for you to decide,” Helen growled at the upperclassman blocking the hallway. The blue sunlight streaming through the large windows to their right provided minimal illumination for the off-worlder Helen due to her refusal to wear lenses adjusting the wavelength, but she still clearly saw it when her adversary sneered at her.

“Everyone’s saying it. It’s obvious you’re never going to make it. People like you aren’t cut out to be officers, and you’re just wasting everyone’s time pretending otherwise,” the blonde woman insisted as she looked down her nose at the slightly shorter redhead.

"Your opinions mean nothing."

"That's fact, not opinion. Now show proper respect for once and salute me."

The last word was barely out of the woman's mouth when Helen's fist slammed into it. The blow spun her towards the wall allowing Helen to shove her facefirst into the row of gray lockers.

Her victim had just enough time to turn around before Helen was on top of her again, pinning her against the lockers with her left hand with the other fist already poised to strike, but the attack never landed.

She cried out in pain and surprise as someone grabbed her arm and wrenched it behind her, then yanked her away and started marching her down the hall. Any other cadets they passed immediately snapped to attention upon seeing them, but she hardly noticed as she fought to free herself from the vice-like grips on her wrist and shoulder.

"Let me go!" she appealed without success.

They burst into the superintendent's office, passed the shocked secretary without saying a word and entered the office proper where she was thrown into a chair facing the desk.

"What is the meaning of this?" General Vise demanded to know as he shot to his feet.

His answer had to wait as Helen attempted to stand up to face her attacker, but a firm hand held her down while the man walked around to face her. It was then that she saw the black uniform of an Azul Guardian, with the green stripe running down the left and blue on the right, and she finally quit struggling. Even she knew that she didn't stand a chance against a member of the union's elite special forces.

"Captain," Vise prodded.

The guardian held Helen for a moment longer as he looked into her eyes, then he released her when he saw she was done fighting and turned towards the general.

"I was on my way to see you, sir, when I spotted this one fighting with another classmate."

"Physically?"

"Affirmative."

The general sighed as he sank back into his chair and looked Helen in the eyes.

"I've heard of your discipline issues, Cadet Dodge, but I hoped you knew better than to take things this far. Do you understand what academy regulations require be done at this point?"

She didn't, but wasn't about to admit that, so she just stared at him. That was until the captain took a step towards her and demanded she answer.

"No, sir."

"Physical violence between students is to result in the immediate expulsion of one or both parties. I'll find out who else was involved and deal with them later, but I'm reasonably certain that your actions merit this penalty."

So her career was over before it even had a chance to start. She'd have to go back home and admit her father was right.

"Do you have nothing to say in your defense?"

It wasn't fair that giving that arrogant brat exactly what she deserved should ruin her whole future, but Helen said nothing out loud and instead looked at the floor as she fought back angry tears.

The general sighed again, then looked at the man who'd brought her in.

"Captain Breise, I assume you are still here because there is something you'd like to add?"

"Thank you, sir, there is. We need all the soldiers we can find to fight the Ordonians, and she has exhibited a fighting spirit if nothing else. I'd like your permission to transfer her to Guardian training. If anyone can teach her discipline, it's us."

Helen couldn't stop herself from looking up at her captor turned advocate in surprise. His dark features gave nothing away as he continued to look towards the general, but she could swear that Vise was just covering up a smile when she glanced his way.

"She would be your responsibility."

"I understand, sir."

The general nodded, then looked back at the young cadet who kept looking back and forth between the two officers.

"You are hereby suspended from this academy until such time as you complete special forces training under the supervision of Captain Peter Briese. Should you fail that training, you will not be allowed to come back or to enlist in any other part of the Vehlan Union military. Is this understood?"

"Yes, sir," Helen responded so quietly it was almost a whisper, then quickly added, "Thank you."

Vehla
Fort Guardian
Monday, November 5th, 2694
5:58 A.M.

The batch of raw cadets, thirty of them at Helen's count, tried not to shiver too much as the rain continued to drench their already soaked bodies and thicken the mud beneath their feet. They'd been ordered to stand there at attention until told otherwise, but an hour of that had many of them already questioning the wisdom of their choice to become Azul Guardians.

Only one instructor stood in front of them, relatively comfortable in his poncho while he watched them fight the elements wearing nothing but t-shirts, loose pants, and boots. Not an ounce of sympathy showed on his face as he focused on one cadet, then another, judging which of them were going to break. Not that anyone could really see his face in the dark anyway.

Finally, another instructor clomped through the mud to stand at center front. He did a quick survey of the class before him, then continued to look them over as he delivered an introductory speech.

"Welcome to Azul Guardian training, an experience that even war competes with to be the worst imaginable to human beings. All of you have chosen to be here, for one reason or another," he began, his gaze settling on Helen in the second line, who was likely given away by her red hair and light skin.

"You can choose to leave at any time without judgement or condemnation. Few have what it takes to live this life, and there is no shame in not being one of them."

The instructor paused and looked around as if waiting for people to realize they'd made a big mistake and leave right then and there, but no one did.

"Most of you are here as enlisted personnel, but some of you are meant to become officers. You are here together because Guardians face everything together. None of you will receive special treatment in combat, so no one gets it in training. We fight together, or we all die."

He took one last look at the young men and women arrayed before him, then nodded at the other instructor before walking off, his pace strong and steady despite the mud sucking his boots down with each step.

5:43 P.M.

Helen rounded the corner with the front of the group and kept pace with them as they slogged back into the training field, finally nearing the end of the ten-mile run. The rain had stopped earlier in the day, but not until after several sets of push-ups, stomach crunches, and aerobics had gotten the cadets well-acquainted with the mud, much of which now covered them from head-to-toe.

The five of them, the first to arrive, jogged up to face the instructor who had been joined by Captain Briese, then snapped off a salute and stood at attention.

"Cadet Dodge, you are dismissed to go with Captain Breise," the instructor revealed. She saluted again, then stepped out of formation and up to the captain.

"Good luck, Breezy," the instructor mumbled as the two turned to walk away.

"Breezy?" Helen ventured to ask once they were out of earshot.

"It's customary for Guardians to be given nicknames by their peers. You'll get one too, if you manage to make it," Breise explained.

He stopped at a solitary chair set beside a warehouse and sat down to face her while she remained standing with hands clasped behind her back.

"Tell me about yourself," he prompted.

She was tired, filthy, hungry and in no mood for small talk, but she did her best to push all that down and respond as cordially as possible.

"There's nothing to tell," she said, then hastily added a sir when he gave her a pointed look.

"As your advisor, I'm suggesting you quit right now and go home."

"What?"

"You don't take orders, and you don't work as part of a team. There's no place for you in this military."

Anyone else she would have knocked out of their chair for talking to her like that, but he was her last chance at the life she wanted, so she clasped her hands even tighter and declared that she would not quit.

"Then tell me about yourself."

There was no hiding the frustration in her voice this time, "I grew up in a farming town on Swarnlia. My father and siblings were unbearable, but I was close to my mother. She died a few months ago, and that's when I decided to join."

"Maybe there's hope for you yet," Breise commented as he rose from the chair. He glanced towards the training field, then instructed her to jog around it until he told her to stop.

The rest of the cadets finished the run during her first lap, and on the second they were dismissed for the day after which they trudged off towards the barracks, too tired to talk or notice the lone cadet still training.

More exercises followed, and then even more after that. Her active childhood meant she was in good shape, but she couldn't keep this up forever.

When she was sure she was about to collapse, the captain told her to stop and stand at ease. The stars were shining brightly overhead to provide passable illumination as Breise just stood there watching her.

"Go get some sleep," he finally ordered.

"What about getting something to eat, sir?"

"The commissary is closed. Since eating would have required you to interact with others, I thought I'd spare you the inconvenience."

Her response was an astonished look, her mouth hanging open in disbelief.

"Think about that come breakfast time. You're dismissed," he stated without sympathy.

She clenched her jaw to keep from saying something snide, then walked off and tried not to think about the painful emptiness in her gut. At least there was enough time to wash off all the gunk and still get a couple hours of sleep.

Unfortunately, Captain Breise had one last thing to say while she was still close enough to hear.

"Oh, the showers are also locked by now."

The words running through her mind were not for the faint of heart.

Vehla
Purgatory Mountain
Saturday, December 6th, 2695
12:22 P.M.

This was it. The final day of the final test. All she had to do now was make it to the extraction point in time and she was in. A year of training culminating in a week in the wilderness, and now mere minutes would determine her final fate.

A scream cut through the woods and she skidded to a stop. She slowed her breathing so as to hear better, and was able to determine the direction upon hearing a shout.

She took off running towards the sound, glancing at the sun as she did so. Not much time left.

There was a break in the trees ahead, so she slowed her pace, then came to a halt at the edge of a sheer cliff. A river frothed over thirty meters below, but a couple meters below her there was a scraggly tree from which another cadet was dangling.

"Is anyone there?" he shouted.

"Yes. I'm here! Can you get a foothold?"

"No! The rocks are too far away!"

These were supposed to be the solo trials, with the team qualifications having been the week before, but there wasn't time to think about that. She hurriedly slipped off her pack, pulled out a rope, and tied one end around a large tree before clipping on and throwing the other end over the cliff.

"Hurry! I don't know how much longer I can hold on!"

"I'm coming!" she snapped as she turned her back to the cliff, took a deep breath, then pushed off.

She reached the other cadet within seconds, but he was too far behind her to grab.

"Can you move closer to the cliff face?"

"I don't know. My hands are already slipping."

"Are you training to be a Guardian?"

"Yeah."

"Then this shouldn't be a problem."

He hesitated a moment as she hung there, her head twisted around as far as it would go so she could see him, but then he finally began shimmying closer.

Once he was close enough, she reached out her left arm and side-stepped along the cliff face until they were side by side, then wrapped the arm around him and held him until he could grab the rope.

She only had the one carabiner, but he was able to get a good grip and climb up as she followed.

"Thank you," he gasped once they were back on firm ground.

"We have to get moving," she insisted and repacked the rope as quickly as she could and donned her pack.

He nodded his understanding, and the two of them took off running.

They reached the extraction point without any more trouble, but the clearing was empty. A steadily decreasing thruster noise indicated the transport had just left.

"I guess that's it then. We failed," Helen's classmate, who she recognized as Ray Kester, moaned as he looked towards the sound.

"So they just left us here?"

"They'll probably come back once our failure has had a chance to sink in," Ray guessed as he sank to a sitting position on the ground, but Helen remained standing and was looking towards the bottom of the mountain.

"I'm not about to wait around for them to decide to come get us. The camp is only a couple hours from here," she declared, then started off in that direction.

"You're going to walk out of here!"

"You're welcome to join me," Helen offered without looking back. She was into the trees before she heard him run up beside her.

"I can't let you go out there alone. You might fall and need someone to help you up," he joked, but she just kept walking.

Purgatory Base Camp
4:07 P.M.

The shadows were growing long as Helen and Ray trudged up to the camp to find Captain Breise waiting for them.

"Took you long enough," he quipped with a smile, the first she'd ever seen from him.

"I prefer to finish things, one way or another," Helen declared.

The captain nodded, then turned to address her companion.

"Good work, Sergeant. You can head back to base whenever you're ready."

"Thank you, sir," Ray responded with a salute, then walked away while Helen watched, too tired to be surprised. When he was gone, she looked to the captain for an explanation.

"We always plant someone in the classes to test recruits in various ways."

"But he caused me to fail the course," Helen complained.

"No, he caused you to pass the course. You may have passed the team trials, but I wanted to make sure you were ready to put aside your personal goals for the sake of others."

She probably would have punched him for that a year ago, but now she just gave a relieved smile.

"Now you get to go back to the academy for three years," he teased.

"And now nobody can stop me from beating up anyone who gets in my way," she joked back, and he laughed as he handed her a bottle of water and led the way to the transport.

Not In My Empire

Binat
Thursday, May 12th, 2698
2:00 P.M.

"The glory of the Ordeon Empire is expressed not only in our ability to conquer our enemies, but also in how we care for our people. The life of every imperial citizen enriches us with constant devotion to the betterment of oneself, the empire, and the entire human race. It is the empire's duty, *my* duty, to show that same devotion to the people when they find themselves in need. We are one people, and when one of us hurts, we all hurt."

Applause erupted from the crowd gathered in the field before the royal transport, and Johan Lentaise, crown prince of the Ordeon Empire, paused in his speech to bask in their adoration. His position halfway up the transport's ramp afforded him a good view of his audience, allowing him to see the love on their faces as they soaked in every word.

"When disaster struck this planet, you requested aid, but that request was lost and forgotten for many years in the midst of the war effort, but no longer. I heard your cry and knew what I must do. I delivered the resources to rebuild and stayed long enough to personally ensure they were being put to the most efficient use possible."

More applause.

"I leave you now to continue my mission to see to the needs of all those who have found themselves forgotten due to the union's aggression, but know that I am never far away. Call upon me should you have the need, and I will come.

"To the future!"

The crowd burst into another round of applause, this time combined with enough cheering and shouting to nearly drown out the live band which played the royal anthem as the prince walked the rest of the way up the ramp with his two Star Knight guards close behind.

"What's our next destination, Penavel?" Johan asked as he settled into a seat at a table and accepted a drink from an attendant.

"Durshon," the knight commander responded, taking the seat across from the prince.

"Durshon? Are the separatists causing trouble again?"

"Unknown. Local agencies report the cells are quiet, but knights passing through the area have heard stories of people disappearing and there are rumors the local law enforcement is failing to do anything about it."

The transport's engines finished powering up, and the craft lifted from the ground and quickly flew into the sky.

"That doesn't sound typical of the separatists. When they abduct someone, it's always a politician whom they hope is important enough to force us to grant concessions. They don't grab random people off the street," Johan observed.

"Agreed. However, the number of disappearances is abnormally high. Something is wrong there."

"Let's review the reports," Johan commanded, and the two of them settled in to work.

Durshon
Friday, May 13th, 2698
8:00 A.M.

Two knights burst into the governor's office and held the doors open for Crown Prince Lentaise and Knight Captain Penavel who were followed by another pair of knights. The knights were wearing their grey trimmed in black semi-formal uniforms, while the prince sported his royal military uniform of dark red pants, double-breasted black jacket with brass buttons, and black combat boots.

Most of the group stopped just inside the door while the prince strode straight up to the desk to stare the now standing governor in the eye.

"Your Highness, I wasn't expecting you today," the governor stammered.

"I've received some disturbing reports about your planet, Governor. You are not doing your job, so I deemed it necessary to personally see to the needs of your people," Lentaise responded.

"I don't understand."

"My knights report a high number of missing persons cases occurring on this planet, far higher than average. Many of them seem to be disappearing from right under your nose in the prison system, with no records to indicate destination or fate. When family members seek help from the authorities, they are ignored. In some cases, they go missing as well."

The blood drained from the governor's face as the prince spoke, and he finally fell into his chair under the weight of the unspoken accusations.

"I await your explanation."

"We have been looking into ways to eliminate the separatists once and for all. A few of our citizens join them every year, and they always stir up trouble once their numbers give them the illusion of safety. It was decided we should learn why people would leave the comfort of civilization to hide in the jungle. We hoped to cut them off so they would wither away and finally die."

"Get to the point."

"A psychological profile was created for every citizen, and our top sociologist was put in charge of the project. We built a new facility for him to conduct his research and began sending him the subjects he requested. He insisted that if the general population knew of the program, it would skew the results and make it nearly impossible to draw a proper conclusion, so we have done what was necessary to keep it a secret."

"How long has this been happening?"

"Over three years."

The prince placed his hands on the desk and leaned forward, holding the governor's eyes with his own.

"None of these people have returned from the facility?" he asked quietly.

The governor could only respond by shaking his head no.

"What happens to them?"

"I don't know."

"You don't want to know," the prince accused, and was validated when the governor nodded and lowered his eyes to the floor in shame.

"Penavel," Lentaise called as he straightened up.

"Sir?"

"Get the location of the facility and take him into custody, then assemble my entire detail and take me there."

Lentaise gave the governor one last disgusted look, then stalked out of the room with three of the knights close behind.

10:00 A.M.

The convoy exited the tunnel formed by the thick jungle surrounding the dirt road and pulled up to the facility, stopping with the prince's door facing the path leading to the main door. Over two dozen Star Knights rushed out of their vehicles and quickly secured the area before their sovereign stepped foot on that path.

The first thing Johan noticed upon stepping out was the gray carbocrete walls surrounding the buildings with regularly spaced guard towers rising up behind them. Such things were not unusual for a government facility located within a jungle known to house people hostile to the empire, but upon looking closely he could see the guards in the towers were watching both the interior and exterior such as they would do in a prison.

"Crown Prince Johan! What an honor!" a well-groomed man in his forties wearing a white lab coat exclaimed as he approached the cars.

"Dr. Wegin, I presume?" Johan observed as the man gave a short bow.

"At your service, Majesty."

Knight Commander Penavel moved up as if he was going to seize the doctor, but Johan stopped him with an outstretched arm. Their actions, and their meaning, seemed to escape Wegin's notice as the enormous smile never left his face.

"Select two knights to accompany us and leave the rest here," Johan whispered to the commander, then turned his attention back to their host.

"I only recently heard of this place and the research you are doing here. I would appreciate a tour."

"It will be my delight to show you around personally," Wegin enthused as he performed another bow. He then turned and led the way to the blast doors which served for a main gate. Once there, he began typing on a terminal in the nearby wall while continuing to speak.

"To be honest, I've been hoping someone from the royal court would come around for an inspection, but I never dreamed it would be the crown prince!"

"I prefer to see things for myself," Johan responded, already wearied by the man's cheerful attitude.

A klaxon sounded as Wegin finished inputting his codes, and the doors smoothly slid to both sides and out of their way, then quickly closed again once they were all through. Johan shot a look at Penavel who signaled one of the accompanying knights to take up position in the nearby guardhouse.

It looked like a normal enough research campus on the inside with doctors in lab coats walking in pairs and groups discussing their latest experiments and tech assistants rushing from one job to another, eager to please their bosses. There were a large number of armed guards around the buildings, but that could be attributed to the secret nature of the program.

However, it didn't escape the prince's notice that several of the employees glanced their way with fearful expressions, and a few guards even tightened their grips on their weapons. He glanced at Penavel to see him tense up and move a hand closer to his own weapon, telling him that he had also noticed.

"What is the purpose of your research?" the prince questioned.

"I seek to identify the genes responsible for anarchistic behavior, then find a way to eliminate them," Wegin replied. As they moved deeper into the facility, the researchers and lab techs thinned out while the guards increased in number.

"I was told you are a sociologist. How are you researching genetics?"

"Hired scientists take care of the lab work. My job is to study their results and find a way to apply the findings to society."

The doctor finally led them into a building, and after a brief biological scan they entered a lab full of test tubes, beakers, and scanning equipment. In the center of the room a young man and woman in hospital gowns lay sedated and restrained on separate tables where a lab tech was currently taking a tissue sample from the man.

"This is where we study our most promising subjects. These two were found by local law enforcement sneaking into the jungle, and it was determined they were on their way to join the separatists. They've already been through extensive psychological examination, and now we are mapping their DNA and comparing it to loyal citizens to find any abnormalities."

"Why are they sedated and restrained?"

"Standard procedure. Our patients are naturally predisposed towards violence, so we do what we must to ensure the safety of our personnel."

They watched as the tech took the tissue sample, placed it in a scanner, then catalogued it and stored it when the scan finished.

After that, Wegin led them through many more buildings, showing them the analysis process of the DNA samples, patients in small rooms being questioned by doctors, and the holding cells.

An hour into the tour, the facility's chief of security caught up with them and pulled the doctor aside to have a hushed conversation with him. The prince and his companions couldn't hear what was said, but it was clear the chief was extremely worried about something and wanted to stop the tour. Wegin refused, sent him on his way, and returned to the group.

Suspicious of the chief's motives, Johan ordered Penavel to keep an eye on him. He didn't want to go and leave his liege with no more than a single guard, but the prince insisted and his order was obeyed.

"This is our last stop, and I hope it will be what convinces you to implement this program nationwide," Wegin finally said as he led them to a large warehouse-type building, his smile growing larger than ever.

"Your problem is a local one, thus your solution is not needed by the rest of the empire," Johan observed.

“You're absolutely right, of course, but I have already made plans for how the program can be expanded so our society as a whole can benefit,” Wegin replied, and the prince nodded, signaling him to continue.

The inside turned out to be one large room, divided down the middle by a thick white, plastic curtain that went about halfway up the wall. In the center of the curtain a booth had been set up using poles and more curtains. There was a line of over a dozen prisoners leading up to the booth, with each one in a green hospital gown, gagged, and bound by the wrists and ankles which forced them to shuffle their feet to move forward with the line. A dozen guards spread around the room kept close watch.

There were no comments from the doctor as he led them to a split in the curtain and held it aside for them to pass through.

There were fewer guards on this side, but there were a few workers dressed in one-piece, grey jumpsuits who were sorting through items on a table and dropping them in bins. On the far wall sat a large plasma furnace, a device capable of vaporizing almost anything.

Two men in similar clothes, but sporting surgical masks, came out of the booth carrying a prisoner on a stretcher. They tipped the motionless body onto an empty table, then returned to the booth while others began stripping the prisoner and placing the gown and restraints on a nearby counter.

“Take care of this,” Johan ordered his remaining knight. His blood was boiling at the sight and he clenched his jaw tight as he headed for the booth while the knight marched towards the workers.

“Highness!” Wegin called out, but the outburst was ignored.

He reached the booth and threw the curtain aside just in time to see a doctor about to inject a teenage boy lying on the metal table in the center.

Johan quickly grabbed the injector out of the doctor's hand and pushed him into the workers with the stretcher. A guard stepped forward to stop him, but the prince knocked his hands away and thrust the injector into his neck. His eyes widened in shock and terror, then he fell to the ground.

"What are you doing!?" Wegin shouted as the prince threw down the injector. Johan's response was to punch him in the jaw, knocking him on his backside.

"What am I doing? What are *you* doing?" Johan exclaimed.

The doctor wiped blood from his mouth and stared at it on his hand, too shocked to respond. Guards tore open the curtain from the other side, weapons at the ready, but they quickly pointed them at the ground once they saw who was causing the commotion.

"Penavel, report," Johan spoke into the communicator attached to his right ear.

"I apprehended the security chief when he attempted to flee and forced him to tell me everything. We have already seized control of the facility, and reinforcements are on their way to you."

"They're not needed. Use them to make sure nobody escapes."

"Yes, sir."

"Do you not know such practices are forbidden by law, and have been for centuries?" Johan questioned Wegin, still lying on the floor by his feet.

"What laws?" Wegin asked, clearly confused. The prince's response was to step towards him as though to kick him, and the doctor quickly backed away in fear.

"Some of the others thought there might be a problem with the laws against genetic cleansing, but that's not what we're doing here!"

"Then what do you think this is!"

"We are identifying rebels and other criminals and executing them before they can cause harm!"

His rage surging, the prince reached down with both hands, grabbed Wegin by the collar and pulled him to his feet.

"You can't know what these people will do!" he shouted into his face.

"Yes, I can. We can. That's what we've been learning to do here!"

"They are imperial citizens, worthy of all the rights, and respect, that entails! We don't judge people for things they *might* do!"

"I have only ever sought to protect our citizens!"

The prince threw him back on the floor and turned away, disgusted, and saw that Penavel had rejoined him.

"Call in every available knight in the region. Any prisoner who has an actual criminal record is to be returned to court for consideration to have their sentences commuted. All others are to be freed without condition. Everyone involved in this atrocity is to be arrested and tried accordingly, and I want this place burned to the ground."

"It shall be done, Majesty."

"Wait! Can't you see it is better to find and eliminate these people before they cause harm?" Wegin pleaded.

"One more word out of you, and I will toss you into that furnace alive."

Saturday, May 21st, 2698
8:23 P.M.

Orange light flickered across the solemn faces of the crowd as the flames consumed the facility. The crown prince was there with his knights, but also in attendance were many of the former prisoners who had been invited to view the conclusion to their suffering along with all of the research personnel who had been forced to come and watch their work burn.

"Such practices were supposed to be eliminated generations ago, Penavel. It causes me great concern to find them in our day," the prince observed.

"We should have learned about this and put an end to it long ago, sire. On behalf of the knights, I offer you our apologies," Penavel responded.

"No, this is not your fault. The Vehlans have distracted us, causing us to allow cancers like this to grow within our own borders. I will end all these evils we are discovering, then I will destroy the Vehlans. Only then will we finally know peace."

Choices Made

Palcion
Monday, July 22nd, 2701
6:53 A.M.

The workers shielded their eyes from the dirt and dust stirred up by the landing transport, but there was nothing they could do to stop it from smearing their white uniforms.

The ship touched down and immediately extended ramps from all sides, then dozens of workers and volunteers rushed in with stretchers and wheelchairs to meet the disembarking passengers, all of whom were covered in blood and filth. Kate Tyquese was one of the first to arrive, and she was met by a medical aide pushing a stretcher.

"Heavy blood loss! Need immediate transfusions!"

"Bus One!" she delegated.

"Lacerations on legs, but bleeding is stopped for now!"

"Bus Three!"

"GSW to shoulder!"

"Bus Five!"

Many more wounded followed, both soldiers and civilians, and she directed each one to the appropriate bus according to the urgency of their injuries. When the ship was finally empty, she climbed into the last vehicle, made sure all patients were secure, and signaled the driver to move out before starting treatment.

Vehlan Patrol Squadron
VUS Halerd
8:32 A.M.

"Detecting two enemy fleets entering the sector!" Tactical shouted.

"Condition Red! Projected destinations?" Captain Lester reacted.

"Palcion and Sherinova!"

The presence of Ordonian fleets in their territory was so common these days that Petty Officer Sam Tyquese didn't pay much attention to the report at first and simply prepared to lay in a new course, but then he heard the names of the planets and froze with hands hovering above his console.

"Set course for Sherinova! Full speed!" Lester ordered.

"What about Palcion, sir?" Sam questioned without inputting the coordinates.

"What about it, Petty Officer?" Commander Winters, the ship's second in command, retorted.

"There are only minimal defenses in that system, sir. Sherinova already has a large fleet presence. Doesn't it make more sense for us to go to the aid of defenseless civilians?"

"I gave you an order, Navigation."

The captain's mind was clearly made up, but Sam's sister was on Palcion. How could he set a course that would take them several hours away from her, likely leaving her to die?

He glanced at the helmsman, but the only response he got was an impatient look, unable to do his job until Sam plotted a course. He considered locking in a course to Palcion anyway, but realized he would never get away with it.

"Course set for Sherinova."

Palcion
9:04 A.M.

"You're going to be okay. A quick surgery, then a couple weeks of recovery, and you'll be good as new. Nothing to worry about," Kate reassured the man on the bed in front of her, smiling and holding his hand. He nodded and weakly returned the smile, but it didn't reach his eyes.

Everything she said was true, but there was no way for her to know what experiences continued to haunt him. His physical injuries would heal quickly, but the emotional wounds would take a lot longer.

"Stay strong," she encouraged him, then gave his shoulder a quick squeeze before moving on to the next patient.

She quickly, but carefully, checked the elderly man's bandages and was about to ask him how he felt, but was interrupted by the city's warning sirens going off.

"What's going on?"

"Are we under attack?"

"Not again."

The whole ward erupted into a flurry of questions, whimpering, and outright crying, and the staff hustled to maintain calm.

"They're going to kill us!" an older woman cried out.

"That's not going to happen. The military won't let it. My own brothers are stationed nearby, and I know they won't let me down," Kate reassured her, but she could only hope it was the truth.

The clinic director finally burst through the main door leading a team of stretcher carriers.

"An Ordonian fleet is headed this way, but there is no need to panic. The early-warning system picked them up, and we have plenty of time to get everyone into the shelter," he explained.

It was odd for the empire to attack a planet with so little strategic value, but there was no time to think about that now. Training and experience kicked in to override all else, and Kate hurried to help get the most critical patients into the bomb shelter in the basement.

She chose the stairs to go back up so as to save the elevator for those coming down, and was still climbing when the building shook violently, nearly sending her tumbling back down, but she gripped the handrail and pulled herself forward.

The bombs were falling.

Sherinova
9:13 A.M.

The soldiers watched the descending imperial transport from their position at the edge of the base where they had taken cover behind some stripped down vehicles. When he could tell where it would be landing exactly, Major Leon Tyquese used hand signals to reposition a few of them, setting up the most efficient killzone possible. Sophisticated jamming equipment prevented the transport's sensors from detecting them, but the soldiers onboard would still know they were close.

Some of the younger soldiers bristled with nervous energy as the ship landed, but they held their fire.

The transport touched down with its front towards the Vehlan base, and twenty drones poured out of the back and formed a line with half on each side. These drones were on treads, and each one sported a metal shield large enough for two men to hide behind with a firing slot near the top.

A platoon's worth of soldiers came next. Some took up position on either side of the drone line, but most took cover behind the shields.

The Vehlans aimed their weapons when the attackers began moving forward, but Leon held up a hand to signal them to wait.

Fingers twitched on triggers and several nervous glances were shot his way, but the major allowed the enemy to move closer and closer to the base.

He waited until they had traversed half the distance, then finally swung his hand forward in one sharp motion.

Dozens of lasers shot out from the piles of junk, cutting down the Ordonians at the edges and forcing the rest to halt their advance to return fire, their white plasma melting metal and igniting small fires in the grass.

A pair of rockets shot out from either side of the Vehlan position and scored direct hits on the center of each line, blasting apart the shields and sending bodies flying. Red laser fire poured into the gaps while more rockets targeted the remaining drones.

A distant, but steadily growing, roar caught Leon's attention, and he looked up to see a heat trail descending through the atmosphere.

"Cover!" he shouted, and his soldiers bent forward with hands on heads as the profile of an imperial bomber revealed itself.

It dropped a bomb and fired a pair of rockets at the defenders. The bomb harmlessly detonated in the field not far in front of Leon, but the rockets scored direct hits farther down the line. Bodies flew in every direction, along with a large amount of shrapnel which embedded itself in whatever got in its way, including people.

Cries of pain and shouts for medics filled the air as the Ordonians reformed their line and continued moving forward, shooting as they went.

"Keep firing!" Leon shouted.

The bomber circled around to make another run, but then two Vehlan Javelin Fighters launched from the base and moved to intercept, forcing it to pull up and head back for its formation.

The Javelins abandoned the pursuit and instead lined up a strafing run on the attacking soldiers who then accelerated their advance in an attempt to get close enough to the defenders to deny the aircraft a clear shot.

"Suppression fire!"

The defenders opened up with everything they had, blasting apart the drones and shattering the Ordonian line to send most of the soldiers dropping to the dirt as a final means of protection. Those who remained standing were quickly gunned down.

Now they were completely exposed to both air and ground fire, and there was no retreat for the normally indomitable Ordonian troops as the Javelins neared firing position, so their commander finally ordered a cease fire and held his rifle in the air. His troops quickly followed suit, so Leon waved off the Javelins then led half his people onto the field with weapons aimed at the imperial soldiers slowly rising to their feet.

Palcion
10:42 A.M.

The bombs and plasma fell on the city like a deadly rain, but Kate ignored them and continued to dig at a pile of rubble. She'd seen someone buried when it fell, and wasn't going anywhere until she got him out.

A boy's head appeared when she moved a piece of concrete aside, and she hastily dug out more to expose his neck so she could feel for a pulse.

There wasn't one.

"Tyquese! Over here!" someone shouted, denying her even a moment of mourning, and she turned to see one of her fellow clinic workers waving at her.

She ran over to find him kneeling over a middle-aged man with a severe gash in his right leg showing through a tear in his blood-soaked pants.

"His leg is broken and he's losing a lot of blood. Help me get him to the clinic."

"I can get there myself. There are others who need help."

"You're not going anywhere by yourself with that leg. Let us help," Kate insisted, and the man nodded his consent.

They took him by the arms and lifted him to his feet, then set out for the clinic, but it was slow going with the patient dragging his bad leg and hopping on the other.

Meanwhile, the bombardment continued, gradually reducing the city into a pile of rubble. At least there weren't any enemy soldiers around to gun them down.

"Why haven't our ships stopped this yet?"

"The nearest patrol squadron was a couple hours away when this started. I'm sure they'll be here soon," Kate answered her friend.

"They'd better."

"There's the clinic. We'll get him some help, then go back out to look for others."

They picked up the pace at the sight of their goal, but then the building exploded and sent the three of them flying.

Kate landed on her side seconds later, searing pain instantly bursting through her body while flaming debris rained down around her.

Dazed but still conscious, she raised her head in an effort to locate her companions, but could not see them.

She tried to stand, but only met with fresh pain.

Then the pain dulled, and a strange peace came over her as she rested her head back on the ground.

She closed her eyes and thought of her brothers, the younger who was the pariah of the family and felt she was the only one who understood him, and the older whose stubborn patriotism blinded him to all else.

"It's all up to you now guys."

VUS Halerd
Sherinova
11:02 A.M.

"Orbital control established. The enemy is in full retreat," Tactical reported.

"Enemy ground forces?" Captain Lester asked.

"Still in play."

"Send reinforcements."

"What about Palcion, sir?" Petty Officer Tyquese inquired without turning away from his console.

"Status of Palcion?"

"Hostiles retreated at the same time as their counterparts here. Significant damage to all major cities," Communications responded.

The breath caught in Sam's throat at the news, and he found himself staring at his console while struggling to breathe.

"What about the relief services?" he managed to choke out.

"Barely operating. They suffered several casualties themselves."

Sam leapt out of his chair and whirled around to face the captain, causing the security guards to instinctively reach for their weapons at his ferocity.

"Captain, I request temporary leave. My sister is a relief worker on Palcion. I have to go find her."

"Request denied. Resume your station."

The denial shocked him, leaving him unable to do anything but stare at the captain in disbelief.

"The captain gave you an order," Winters declared.

"But she's my sister."

“We all have family in dangerous situations. If we took leave every time one of them might be hurt, there wouldn't be anybody left to fight. Now resume your station,” Lester insisted.

Still unable to believe what he was hearing, the petty officer looked around at the other bridge officers, but found all of them pretending the conversation wasn't even happening.

Then he looked back at the captain and commander, and felt every muscle in his body tighten when he saw their callous expressions.

“Screw you! I'm going!” he shouted and started towards the main lift.

“Security!”

A pair of guards grabbed him by the arms and held him tight despite his efforts to fight them off.

“Confine him to the brig pending charges of insubordination,” Lester commanded, and the guards dragged him away.

Sherinova
12:09 A.M.

Leon leaned against a tree as he watched his soldiers round up the last of the surrendering Ordonians, taking a moment to catch his breath while he could. They had successfully defended the planet with minimal casualties and damage, and that was a fact worth savoring.

“Major Tyquese?” an unfamiliar voice interrupted his musings, and he looked towards the source to see a young lieutenant in a fresh uniform.

“What is it?” he questioned worriedly, pushing away from the tree to stand in front of him.

“The colonel thought you should know that the Ordonians hit Palcion at the same time they attacked here. They conducted an orbital bombardment, and the death toll is thought to be in the hundreds of thousands.”

"What else did he say?"

"A platoon has been made available for you to take to Palcion and assist in the relief efforts."

"Thank you. You're dismissed," Leon responded, then returned the lieutenant's salute before fast walking away.

As he walked, he used his palco to order the platoon to board a transport for immediate departure. Almost as an afterthought, he logged into the fleet network to send a message to his brother only to find out that his ship was part of Sherinova's reinforcements which led to his discovery that he was currently under arrest for insubordination.

He rolled his eyes, then sent orders to the platoon transport to meet him at Sam's ship before going in search of a smaller craft to take him up.

VUS Halerd
1:23 P.M.

The cell door hissed open, and Sam looked up to see his fully armored brother stepping inside.

"What do you want?"

"Some respect would be a good start," Leon told him, and Sam snorted in response.

"I heard what happened, and managed to get them to release you into my custody."

"Am I supposed to be grateful you actually chose to care about your family instead of this stupid war for once?"

"I'm not here to bicker with you, Sam."

"Fine. Then let's get to Palcion and find Kate," Sam retorted as he made his way towards the door, but Leon put out an arm to stop him.

"We're not going to Palcion. We're going home. To Vehla," he revealed, looking deep into Sam's eyes as he spoke.

"Why would we...," Sam started to ask, but then he saw the sadness in Leon's eyes and realized the truth.

Despair and grief threatened to overwhelm him, but then blind rage swept over him instead, and he stepped away from Leon to face the wall.

"How?"

"She was out searching for wounded even while the bombs were still falling, and was returning to her clinic when it was hit."

His fingernails threatened to draw blood as Sam clenched his fists, but he barely noticed.

"We should have been there. I told the captain we needed to protect them, but he ignored me."

"Sherinova was the real target, and what had to be protected. Palcion was only a distraction," Leon argued, causing Sam to smash a fist into the wall.

"Our sister is dead because those who were supposed to protect her cared more about protecting themselves, and you cite strategy to me!"

"You don't understand. You've never understood," Leon sighed, and Sam whirled to face him. He advanced on him as if to hit him, but the older brother just stared at him calmly.

"Forget it," Sam finally concluded, then stormed out of the cell.

Vehla
Thursday, July 25th, 2701
11:30 A.M.

The mourners slowly filed past the closed coffin, some crying while the rest maintained a cold silence. They expressed their condolences to Leon as they passed him in the honor guard, but he only nodded silently while keeping his eyes on Sam.

The youngest member of the Tyquese family hadn't spoken a word, not even to his own family, and glared daggers at anyone who approached him.

When the last guest had paid his respects, Leon dismissed the honor guard and quickly made his way to his brother before he could escape.

"Kate believed in helping people, and she died acting on that belief. Can any of us ask for better?"

"She died because our leaders care more about winning this war than keeping our people safe."

"The only way our people will ever be safe is to defeat the Ordeon Empire. They are the ones who killed all those people; they are the ones deserving of your anger, not us."

"You will never understand," Sam responded, then walked away before another word could be said.

As Leon watched him leave, their parents came up on either side of him, their father limping slightly on his artificial leg.

"I find it hard to believe he is even my son," he commented.

"He's made his choice. There's nothing we can do about it now," their mother added.

"I'll keep an eye on him. He'll come around eventually," Leon assured them.

Victory by Any Means

Ordeos
Ordeos Prime
Tuesday, July 15th, 2702
1:32 P.M.

"Yet another defeat. We will lose this war soon if we continue in this fashion," Crown Prince Johan Lentaise lamented after finishing the latest report from the front.

"Your father is handling the situation," Knight Commander Penavel assured him.

"That doesn't appear to be good enough," Johan declared as he stood up then walked around the desk and went out to his office's balcony. The knight followed, but he scarcely noticed.

The sun warmed his face as he looked past the walls of the palace and military districts to the city beyond which was too far for him to hear its activity, but the light breeze which ruffled his robes did bring with it the sound of voices one floor above. He listened as his children's instructor told them about how the Ordeon Empire was the perfect civilization which would one day lead all of humanity into realizing its full potential.

These were words the crown prince had heard all his life, and now the sentiment was being passed on to his own children, but as his gaze fell to the military district and the soldiers upon the city walls, he couldn't help but wonder if it would ever be anything more than words or a dream.

The imperial people had worked for five-hundred years to make it a reality, but they seemed no closer to their goals now than when they started. There were always anarchists to stand in their way, and the latest war which was meant to finally remove them once and for all was nearing its hundredth year with no end in sight.

"My grandfather started this war but never found a way to finish it, and now my father is repeating his mistakes. It's time to break the cycle. My children will see the future, and rule over it," Johan declared, then turned and headed back inside.

"What is your plan?" Penavel questioned as he fell into step beside him.

"You have served me well for many years and you will be rewarded, but you cannot help me with this. This task and its burden falls to me alone. Leave."

OES Supremacy
Thursday, July 17th, 2702
9:47 A.M.

"Prepare your ship for battle, Captain," Crown Prince Johan announced as he strode onto the bridge with a flourish, flanked on either side by an armored Star Knight, then waited impatiently as the crew completed an obligatory bow. For this occasion, he had chosen to dispense with his royal robes and don his military dress uniform instead.

"I mean no offense, Highness, but this dreadnaught is the personal warship of the emperor. We deploy only at his command," Captain Alvin protested.

"He will issue that command soon, and I want you to be ready when it comes."

"I require confirmation of that order, sir."

"I am the crown prince. My word is all you need, unless you intend to accuse me of being a liar and go straight to my father," Johan threatened.

The captain stiffened as he took a deep breath, then he barked out orders to his crew to ready the ship for combat.

"I will now conduct a personal inspection of this ship. It has been some time since you were deployed, and I must ensure that optimum functionality has been maintained."

"You will find everything is in order, Highness."

"That is for me to decide. I will begin with your communications array as it is vital the emperor be in contact at all times," Johan stated, then walked off the bridge without waiting for a response.

The array was one corridor down from the bridge and he arrived to find the room empty, so he told the knights to wait outside. It was a circular room in the center of which was a thick column with a flared top and bottom which housed the communications equipment.

He first went up to the main console which was in full view of the open door and called up a diagnostic program. On the pretense of waiting for the scan to finish, he walked around to the other side where he opened up an access panel, exposing a myriad of circuits.

The circuit he wanted was near the back of the compartment, behind another one, so he released the clip on one side of the one in front and swung it down, careful to make sure it remained connected to the system. Next, he pulled a small disc from his right pocket, attached it to the back of the target circuit, then put everything back together and returned to the main console.

The diagnostic concluded minutes later to reveal no abnormalities, so he set the system back to normal operations and moved on to the next area on his inspection.

Friday, July 18th, 2702
7:07 P.M.

The crown prince strode past the emperor's secretaries and right into his father's office to find him hunched over his desk, staring at the digital display with head in hands and brow deeply furrowed.

"You can cease your labors, Father. I know what needs to be done," Johan announced, and Calin Lentaise looked up just enough to meet his gaze.

"Do you presume to understand this war better than I do?" he questioned with more weariness than anger.

"On the contrary, I believe it is your expertise which will end our current misfortune and put us firmly back on the path to victory."

The emperor sighed, signaled his son to close the door, then leaned back as he waited for him to come forward and explain himself.

"Our commanders at the front are the ones who continually fail to resist the Vehlan attacks, then they compound their failure by fleeing," Johan accused.

"They act according to my orders," Calin interrupted with a touch of anger.

"Yes, but it is their responsibility to lead on the battlefield, and that is where they falter. When that happens, you are too far removed from them to correct their errors, and the battle is already lost by the time you do."

"What are you suggesting?"

"Take a fleet and personally lead it against the Vehlan incursion. You are the only one who can stabilize the front lines and solidify the confidence of our people."

The emperor fixed his son with a thoughtful stare and did not reply for some time, long enough for Johan to begin fearing where those thoughts were taking him.

"I am surprised that you did not volunteer yourself to command this fleet. You have always been ambitious, and such an action would gain you much favor with the people," Calin finally admitted, his voice betraying no emotion.

"All things must happen in their proper time. There are many years remaining in your reign and I must not risk overshadowing you in the eyes of the people. They need to believe in their emperor, not a prince," Johan clarified.

"Perhaps it is necessary for me to personally resolve this issue, but I require more ships than are currently at the front," Calin mused as he leaned forward to gaze once more at the tactical maps displayed on his desk.

"I have already arranged it. Now that the pirates have been driven out of the territories outside Binat and Tikas, we can spare the ships from those sectors. Your fleet is assembling at Jimlian as we speak."

"Order Primary Lanzis to meet me there as well, and you will act as regent until my return."

"The future belongs to us, and nothing will stand in our way," Johan concluded.

7:34 P.M.

This is necessary. Our destiny cannot be put at risk any longer, Johan reassured himself as he left his father's office.

Now that the emperor had spoken, the prince headed for his own office where he would finalize the tactical arrangements.

The plan was now in motion. He would soon be emperor, and then he would finally finish this war.

Nothing could stand in the way of victory, not even his own father.

Monday, July 28th, 2702
5:06 A.M.

Deep within the palace, the tactical center was full not only with dozens of operators at their stations, but also with the robed crown prince, uniformed master knight, and all seven royal advisors in suits sitting or standing at the central station. The staff worked quietly, speaking in hushed tones, while the royal council watched the wall display which showed the emperor's fleet nearing the Raxin system.

"They have entered normal space and Emperor Calin is signaling for the Vehlan's surrender," the center's commander reported, and Johan had to resist rolling his eyes. A surrender demand was pointless, and he should have opened fire while he still had some element of surprise.

The Vehlans raced towards the Ordonians and both sides opened fire.

Each fleet held steady at first, but it didn't take long for them to notice a clear pattern in the enemy attack.

"They know which ship the emperor occupies!" an advisor blurted out.

"They're trying to kill him, and don't even care about the rest of the fleet!" another exclaimed.

On the screen, the most powerful of the Vehlan ships drove deep into the imperial formation while their fighters and smaller vessels shielded them from incoming fire.

"He has to withdraw!"

"My father would never do something so cowardly. He will find a way," Johan stated calmly.

The Vehlans reached the center of the Ordonian fleet and spread out around the emperor's dreadnaught, ignoring all else and focusing their firepower on the one ship. Not even an imperial dreadnaught could withstand such an assault for long.

They pulled together into a tight formation, blocking any escape for the emperor and preventing any ships from replacing his rapidly dwindling escort. The rest of the fleet formed up around them and fired everything they had, but the enemy stood firm.

"Vehlan defensive technology has always been superior to our own," an advisor murmured, and the crown prince took note of which one.

The seconds agonizingly ticked by as they watched helplessly, waiting for their monarch to turn the battle around or at least find a way to survive, but it became clear there was nothing he could do.

The prince saw it in his periphery as the master knight tapped the sensor on his right wrist which activated a comlink to the emperor's personal guard regardless of location.

"Get to an escape pod!"

All in the room were silent. Some stared at the screen as the damage mounted on the emperor's ship, silently pleading for a miracle. Others watched the master knight, hoping for some word on their monarch.

"Hello! Is anyone receiving?"

Johan turned to look at him, and saw from his expression that he wasn't getting any response.

Then the dreadnaught's symbol disappeared in a flash, and the Vehlans turned their attention towards the rest of the fleet.

"Were any pods launched? Is there any indication of survivors?" Johan choked out, surprising himself at the emotion constricting his voice.

"Negative, Majesty. The ship is totally destroyed, and there is no possibility of survivors," the tactical center's commander responded sullenly.

It seemed as if time itself came to a halt. No one could tear their eyes away from the screen, and the only sound was faint sobbing from a few of the operators.

Then Johan broke the silence when he saw the remainder of their fleet, now leaderless and demoralized, breaking apart under the enemy assault.

"Signal them to fall back."

Whispers began circulating as the initial shock wore off, and the advisors exchanged multiple glances with one another as if none had a clue what to do now, then their gazes settled on the master knight as he stepped forward and knelt before the crown prince to hold up his sidearm and insignia.

"It is the duty of the Star Knights to protect the emperor, and for the first time in history we have failed to do so. Our oath states that if an emperor should be killed, we must die as well. As Master Knight, I name this failure as mine alone and accept the consequences on behalf of all knights."

"The code only requires this if the emperor dies on your watch, and those who were watching him are now dead. You were here, thus you are not responsible for what happened," Johan disputed.

"I respectfully disagree, Highness. The failure of any knight ultimately rests upon me, and I should have better prepared for this circumstance."

The crown prince studied the man kneeling before him, dragging out his final decision for the benefit of the advisors watching both of them, but he had made his decision long before even entering this room.

"Go and execute your final duty. Only you will bear this shame, and the restored honor that will follow," he finally decreed.

"Thank you, Highness."

After the master knight left, Johan stood and told the chief advisor to begin preparing the funeral and coronation.

Monday, September 1st, 2702
6:00 A.M.

All was quiet as the crown prince walked out of the gate into the unlit arena touched by the first rays of dawn, his wife beside him, her hand resting lightly on his left arm. Two-hundred thousand people rose to their feet in the stands while a camera drone hovered before them, relaying the image of the royals in their finest red, white, and yellow robes to the giant monitors on either side of the stadium and to billions of people across the empire.

No one else accompanied the pair, and they kept their eyes straight ahead as they strode purposefully towards center field. Halfway to their destination, they paused at an altar surrounded by roses, a tribute to the late emperor. Atop the altar rested an empty coffin, and they each placed their free hand upon it and bowed their heads.

"I know the truth," Prailia whispered.

"The only truth which matters is the future I will build," Johan insisted. She didn't say anything else, and he knew she wouldn't do anything, so he returned his attention to the ceremony.

They stayed at the altar with heads bowed, aware of nothing but the aroma of the roses and the polished wood under their hands, until the area around them had visibly brightened, then they resumed their march.

The sun rose above the arena wall, bathing the assembly in a golden glow as the royals ascended the ten steps to the stage where they found seven men in yellow robes awaiting them, three at each side and one in the center.

His wife Prailia released his arm, and he continued forward alone until he stood at the opposite edge beside the hierarch, leader of the monastic order dedicated to the empire's purpose. These men and women spent their entire lives in seclusion, centering themselves on the ideal of the perfect civilization so they could watch and intervene if the empire took the wrong path, an action yet to be taken.

The only time any of them left their isolation was to crown a new emperor, the task for which they had assembled this day.

On the sandy ground before the stage stood twenty-one men and women of various ages, heights, skin and hair colors, all with hands clasped behind their backs. These were the governors of each star system in the Ordeon Empire come to pledge their allegiance to the new emperor, including the one from the enemy held territory of Raxin.

“Kneel,” the hierarch commanded in a gruff voice, and Johan got down on both knees. The camera hovered above him to create the appearance of him humbling himself before the Ordonian people.

The elderly hierarch came up to his left side, close enough for the prince to see him in his periphery but without obstructing the people’s view. He held his hands high, his yellow robes billowing around him as he centered the eight-spiked crown with rubies at top and base of each spike over the prince’s head.

“As the chosen of the Lentaise bloodline, it is your responsibility to lead us into the future envisioned by the first emperor, your ancestor Haiden Lentaise. A future free of war, disease, poverty, and all the ills known by humanity today and in ages past. Is this your vision, not only for the people of this nation, but for all humanity?”

“It is.”

“Do you accept this responsibility?”

“I do.”

“As emperor, you will wield total power. Your word will be law, and your commands will be obeyed. This power is given to you to be used in service to the people, to protect and uplift them, not to oppress them for your own glory. Do you recognize and accept this duty?”

“I am one man who will live and rule until death claims me. The empire is eternal, its cause immortal, and sustained by its people. My heart belongs to them.”

“Then I crown you Emperor Johan Lentaise. May your reign be prosperous, and may it at last bring us all the peace and glory we desire,” the hierarch concluded, then gently placed the crown upon Johan’s head, the gold standing out in sharp contrast to his black hair.

He stood up in response to a command from the hierarch and stepped aside as Prailia stepped forward and knelt down as he had. The oath was repeated, the words changed in deference to her not being of Lentaise blood, then a smaller silver crown with five spikes and rubies was set to rest atop her long, golden hair.

The hierarch stepped to center left, making space for Johan to come up beside his wife as she rose after which she rested her hand on his arm again.

"Citizens of the Ordeon Empire, greet your emperor and empress!" a herald announced over the stadium speakers and the crowd erupted into applause and cheers as the governors bowed before the royals.

The new emperor and empress smiled and waved to the crowd in the stands and also to the camera now facing them at eye level, both of them buoyed by the thought of billions of people cheering their coronation.

Now I have everything I need to establish the empire across the entire galaxy, Johan thought as he looked over the crowd.

The future is ours.

Heart of a Survivor

RPS Renegade
Thursday, July 6th, 2705
3:27 P.M.

"Any other contacts?" Lieutenant Sam Tyquese checked as he absentmindedly adjusted the red band on his upper right arm. Their target had entered sensor range, but all they could see was the standard escort for a merchant convoy this size. With how many times they'd attacked this route, one would think the company would have increased security by now.

"Negative," Tactical replied.

The lieutenant leaned forward, his dark features working their way into a scowl as he studied the tactical map displayed on the main screen. There were no unusual power readings or energy fields to indicate anything other than the usual cargo on the transports or standard weapons on the escorts, but that did little to ease his doubts.

"Switch to visual," he ordered, and the screen switched to a view of the convoy, the dark grey ships standing out in clear contrast to the creamy colors of hyperspace.

Once again, he saw nothing unusual. They were calmly flying in a typical formation, apparently totally unaware of an impending attack and unconcerned about the possibility. The jammer vessel was hiding the raiding party from sensors, so it made sense that their victims knew nothing about their presence, but they still should have been on alert.

"They'll be leaving optimum range in less than a minute," Tactical reported, causing Sam to sigh and lean back in his chair.

His instincts were telling him to leave, but he couldn't go back to the captain empty-handed just because he had a bad feeling.

"Send in the Stingers. Deactivate the jamming field the moment they're in range. Fire at will. Screen to tactical."

He could hear the rustling of clothes and impacts of fingers on consoles as the officer rushed to relay his orders, then the screen switched back to the grid to show their ten assault fighters already descending on the four transports and eight escort fighters, each one nearly half the size of their pirate counterparts.

The Stingers strafed the escorts as they flew overhead, but did no damage since most of their power generation was going to the shields to protect against the extreme radiation of hyperspace.

The convoy ships suffered from the same problem, rendering them unable to defend themselves, so they disappeared into normal space only to reappear within star-studded blackness when the pirates followed, after which Sam ordered a general broadcast channel opened.

"You are surrounded by superior firepower. Surrender your cargo and no one will be harmed."

"We do that and we don't get paid," a young male voice responded. Sam swiveled his chair around to glance at his tactical officer whose thin, pale face echoed his confusion.

The answer to demands such as the one he just made was always an agreement to surrender or gunfire. Since when did Merchant crews try reasoning with raiders?

"Which do you prefer? Losing your pay or your life?" Sam responded as he turned back towards the main screen.

His gunship had settled into a firing position above the convoy and the Stingers had surrounded it, but their opponents hadn't done anything except stop all forward motion.

"I can't afford to default on this contract. I'll lose everything if I do," the voice pleaded, but Sam's response was to cut the channel with the press of a button on the arm of his chair.

"They're stalling! Full retreat!" he ordered, but it was already too late.

A patrol cruiser twice their size suddenly appeared behind them, along with twenty more fighters around the perimeter. Fifteen of them were just more escort fighters, but five were the heavier Blacksword fighters used by both private companies in the Merchant's Interest and the Vehlan Union military. More than enough to outmatch Sam's little raiding party.

"This is Captain Anson to pirate raiders. Surrender and prepare to be boarded."

The jammer vessel, which had kept hidden by surrounding itself with a jamming field, fled into hyperspace while most of the Stingers turned and opened fire on the newcomers without orders. Sam ordered the rest to do the same since he didn't want to go to prison any more than they did.

His first instinct was to break through the fighter formation and flee, but they would never outrun the patroller, so he ordered a sweeping turn which narrowly avoided the first volley and brought them around to face their attacker. They scored direct hits with the laser cannon, both laser guns, and both missile launchers, but did very little damage to the other ship's shields.

They had little chance of overcoming the superior vessel, but he wasn't about to go down without a fight.

The Renegade shook from multiple impacts, but Sam hardly noticed it as he ordered Helm to keep them circling the cruiser at high-speed while Tactical continued firing all weapons.

Three of their Assault Fighters were already gone without any losses incurred by the enemy, but the rest he ordered to form up and join the gunship against the cruiser. If they knocked it out of commission, it would be easy enough to escape the fighters.

The convoy had already returned to hyperspace, their schedule preventing them from sticking around to see the outcome of the battle, but Sam's only concern at this point was getting out alive.

"Continuous fire! Divert all available power to weapons and shields, including everything from life-support and as much as you dare from the engines!" he barked out orders.

Even over the noise of battle, he heard the ventilation system quit at the same time the lights went out to leave the bridge lit only by the lights from the control consoles.

The shaking from weapon impacts grew considerably less as their shields surged with fresh energy. The emitters wouldn't take the strain for long, but the flaring shields of their opponent promised they wouldn't have to.

Five more Stingers were shot down by opposing fighters while the patroller focused it's firepower on the Renegade, and Sam clenched his teeth as he watched his ship's shield strength indicator steadily dropping.

Then the cruiser's shields burst in a flash of light, and he ordered Helm to set course away from the battle.

"Target their engines!" he shouted back at Tactical.

The gunship turned away from their enemy, but not before a final barrage could strike the unshielded thrusters and destroy them.

"All power to engines! Jump to hyperspace as soon as we're clear!"

Their weapons powered down and shields dropped to minimum, then Sam was pressed into his seat by acceleration too high for the dampers to completely nullify and the ship raced away from the battlefield with the enemy fighters still following like a swarm of gnats but quickly falling behind.

Then white replaced the blackness and their speed leveled off.

One last glance at the tactical display showed that only one of their fighters had managed to escape with them, and he sullenly ordered course for home.

"Red Castien is going to answer for this," he muttered under his breath.

Altaius
Red Base
Saturday, July 8th, 2705
9:17 A.M.

The guards did nothing as Sam burst through the office door, and the leader of the red faction only glanced at him before returning his attention to his desktop display.

"I hope you know that the cost of the lost fighters and the repairs to your own ship are coming out of your cut," Castien remarked.

"Bite me," Sam spat as he advanced on the desk, his breathing steady despite the sweat dripping on his face and soaking his clothes after his march from the landing pad.

"That is not an acceptable form of payment, but you can earn your percentage back faster if you pay me back from what you already have."

"What's the price of the dead pilots?" Sam jeered.

"Nothing. The dead don't get paid," Castien answered flippantly, having still not looked up, but then Sam slammed both hands on the desk which finally earned him the man's attention.

The captain glanced past him towards the door, but Sam didn't care what the guards were doing and kept his gaze locked on the creep in front of him.

"We shouldn't have attacked the same shipping lane three times in a row, and never five times back-to-back. It's your fault those men are dead," he accused, causing the captain to stand up so fast he sent his chair careening into the wall behind him.

"Those shipments were too lucrative to ignore. It was your job to steal them, so don't blame me for your failure."

"You're too lazy to come up with a proper plan and too stupid to learn to do better!" Sam retorted, nearly shouting now.

The captain leaned to within inches of Sam's face, his breath still stinking of his breakfast, and delivered his next words in a nearly inaudible tone.

"Another comment like that, and I will have you thrown out the airlock of your own ship. Now get out and start figuring out how you're going to pay what you owe me."

Sam held his gaze while he decided if it was worth getting in a final word, but then he just pushed off from the desk and stomped out of the room.

The Den
10:04 P.M.

The building filled with men and women displaying armbands of various colors was a prefabricated structure with one large room that wrapped the three sides of a bar in the center.

It was an unavoidably rambunctious place, but full-on fights were rare. The greens had the connections for bringing in the best booze so all customers made sure to get along regardless of faction. Half the lights didn't work, the floors, walls and ceiling were all covered in stains, and no two pieces of furniture matched, but nobody was there for the decor.

Amid all the bustle, three red pirates sat at a table doing little more than staring into their cups.

"Why do we take orders from that guy?" one of them griped.

"Because the last time I checked, the title was Red Castien, not Red Jake," Sam jabbed as he gave his helmsman a pointed look.

"I'm not sure the title fits anymore," the third one remarked before draining his beer. He then shook it at a woman wearing a white armband to request another.

"If you're talking like that, maybe you shouldn't have any more," Sam suggested to his tactical officer, his own whiskey largely untouched.

"Not like anyone here cares what I think," Gary mumbled as he accepted a fresh bottle from the waitress and took a swig.

"Aren't those the guys that nearly got themselves killed the other day?" a nasally voice cut through the racket and Sam turned to see a group of four guys with yellow armbands looking at them.

"Yeah, they are."

"I heard they kept attacking the same convoy over and over again. What did they think was going to happen?"

"Even we know better than to do that."

"Yeah, I thought the reds were supposed to be smart."

"You got a problem?" one of them challenged when he realized Sam and crew were staring at them, but none of them responded.

"Guess they're too scared," another yellow quipped. Jake shot to his feet, but Sam grabbed his wrist to stop him from doing anything and their mockers walked away laughing.

"Not even the yellows are scared of us anymore," Gary sighed as Sam pulled the younger man back down.

"That proves we're even weaker than I realized, and if something isn't done soon, we'll never recover," Sam mused, and both his companions locked eyes on him.

"Like what?" Gary asked.

"Have our crew back on the ship by eight o'clock," Sam instructed, then got up, paid their tab at the counter, and left with a new determination to his gait.

RPS Renegade
Sunday, July 9th, 2705
8:00 A.M.

Forty-seven men stood in front of Sam in the ship's cargo bay, some of them still looking a little sickly from drowning their sorrows the night before and all of them disheveled as if having just woke up. There should have been fifty, twenty-five crew and twenty-five soldiers for boarding actions, but the missing members were killed in the last engagement.

"Our last raid has shown us just how little our captain cares about us along with his inability to form a proper strategy. This empty cargo bay goes to show just how far we have fallen," he began, then waved his arm around the room to illustrate his last point.

A couple of them followed the gesture and looked around as if noticing the lack of supplies for the first time, but most simply nodded in agreement.

"I have been forced to conclude that if this goes on for much longer, our faction will shrivel up and die, but I've decided that I'm not going to let that happen. I intend to replace Castien as captain of the red faction, and I am asking for your support."

Everyone immediately raised their fists towards the ceiling and shouted their allegiance, although a couple still looked ready to throw up. Some of them even began to switch their armbands from right to left to indicate their membership of a splinter faction, but Sam called on them to wait.

"We need to recruit more to our side before we can make our move. I am granting you a week's leave to do exactly that. Only talk to people you can trust, or at least ones you know are as fed-up with Castien as we are. If he learns of this too soon, we'll do more damage than good.

You're dismissed," he concluded, and they quickly filed out through the two doors behind Sam, all except one.

"You know that the greens will learn of this and sell that information to Castien," Gary warned.

"I'll deal with them. You make sure this ship is ready for a fight," Sam insisted, and Gary responded with a mock salute before slinking off towards the bridge.

Well, he was committed now, for good or bad.

Green Base
Monday, July 10th, 2705
11:12 A.M.

The guard to the left of the office door finally opened it, so Sam rose from the padded chair and strode through, closing it behind him before going up to the desk behind which was seated a short man with a green skull and crossbones pin on his shirt collar.

"You claim to have information to sell me?" Captain Simon Turley questioned.

"No. I have information to give you knowing you would learn of it on your own anyway so I can be here to buy your silence," Sam corrected.

"So you're planning to do something you don't want others to know about. What is it?"

"I intend to replace Red Castien."

"It's about time someone did."

"What will it cost for you not to inform him?"

"Nothing."

"I don't understand," Sam confessed as he stiffened up and looked around the office. Could it be that Green Simon had already learned this, sold it to Castien, and set a trap for him?

"You are in no danger. Castien is weak and should have been replaced a long time ago. The reds stand between the black faction and the rest of us, so it is in all our best interests that you remain strong," Simon explained.

"I'm glad you understand the situation," Sam responded as he relaxed -- slightly.

"There is something else you may be interested in purchasing, however."

"What's that?"

"The price is all of Castien's valuables."

"I need that to rebuild. Name something else."

"That's my offer. Refuse it at your own peril."

It was possible the man was only trying to extort something from him, but that seemed unlikely. He could have made the same demand in exchange for not betraying him to Castien, and he had a reputation for dealing with people fairly, so Sam knew he dare not risk leaving here without the information the captain deemed so valuable.

"Your own attack forces fall short of us in terms of strength, which tends to cause you trouble on the occasion you do decide to conduct your own raids. Tell me what you know, and I will make my forces available to you for two such raids," he finally offered.

Now it was Simon's turn to stop and think. He leaned back in his chair and gazed at his visitor, his face completely inscrutable.

"Five raids, and everything we take belongs to me."

"Three."

"I said five."

Sam took a deep breath, sighed, then nodded in agreement.

"Black Lucius is planning a full-scale attack against your faction with the intent to wipe you out. I don't know when he will strike, but my source says it will be soon."

"Then I will have to move fast, but this should help me gather support," Sam mused, then nodded his thanks to the captain before leaving.

Red Base
Thursday, July 27th, 2705
7:43 P.M.

The mutineers hadn't run into trouble finding volunteers, and now over half the faction had pledged allegiance to Sam Tyquese. Red Castien still had no knowledge of his imminent downfall, and the fact that all the splinter faction sergeants and lieutenants were meeting in the armory of his main base was further proof of the man's incompetence.

Regardless of their good fortune so far, Sam still wished he could take more time to get as many of the rest on their side as possible so they could push out Castien without bloodshed, but there wasn't any time left. The greens had contacted him, for a fee of course, with news that Black Lucius planned to attack within the next couple days, and he needed to get rid of Castien before that happened.

"Is everything set?" he asked Gary who was acting as his second-in-command.

"Almost all of tomorrow morning's guard shifts are filled with our people, and all loyalist Stingers and gunships have been sent elsewhere."

Sam nodded, then turned to address the dozen others gathered with them.

"Lieutenants, make sure your crews know that they are not to fire without my express order. We are doing this to ensure our survival, not to get rich or exact revenge."

The gunship commanders nodded their understanding, so he went on to his final instructions.

"I will signal the beginning of our attack by firing a rocket into the air. When that happens, everyone who is with us is to switch their armbands, then subdue anyone who doesn't. Kill them if you have to, but only if there is no other choice."

He detected a few disappointed looks, but once again everyone nodded their agreement.

"This is our best chance to save our faction from destruction and return it to prosperity. Remember that, and we won't fail."

Friday, July 28th, 2705
7:57 A.M.

In a show of brashness, Sam walked right up to the dirt lot in front of the command center in full view of the door guard who was not among his supporters. He watched with only slight interest as the two pirates with Sam set up a small rocket of a type the Ordonians used for crowd control, one of several they'd stolen over the years but had little use for other than the occasional entertainment.

When they were finished, he made a show of checking his watch while pointing his free finger in the air, then swung the finger down.

They fired the rocket, and it flew straight up several meters before exploding into hundreds of sparks with a sharp report.

He glanced at the door guard, but he still didn't seem to care. For all he knew, Sam was just bored and messing around.

But then over a dozen pirates with armbands on the left arm ran into the lot and rushed the door, and he instinctively aimed his rifle at them, but then quickly dropped it and threw his hands in the air.

Sam and his two companions calmly switched over their armbands, then drew their pistols and stormed into the command center with the others.

No one they encountered tried to stop them, and a few even switched sides to run with them.

They caught up with Castien in a hallway near the back exit and one of the men with him opened fire, wounding one of Sam's men, but then Castien stepped forward with his hands at chest height and palms forward before anyone else could shoot.

The mutineers came to a stop at a signal from Sam, and Castien smiled when he stepped forward.

"What do you expect to accomplish with this, Tyquese? Everyone knows you don't have what it takes to lead," he mocked.

"Clearly they think better of my abilities than yours," Sam responded with a sweeping gesture at all those with him.

"There's only one way to resolve this. If you think you are strong enough to lead these idiots, then prove it by facing me in a duel."

"I've already won. Why would I waste time and energy with a duel."

"It's how upstarts like you used to earn the title of captain. Many pirates still respect that tradition and might not want to follow you otherwise. Of course, you can admit you're too scared to lead and end this stupidity."

"I accept your challenge," Sam declared and holstered his pistol.

9:29 A.M.

As many pirates as could fit had assembled in the training yard around the two duelists, almost all of them now sporting red bands on their left arms. Sam had a feeling that even if he failed this duel, someone else would step up and finish what he had started.

A few were injured in the earlier fighting, but no one was killed which brought the hope of an easy transition since no one had reason to seek revenge.

The spectators formed a ring around the captain and his challenger, both of them armed with a combat knife and shirtless to symbolize their current status as equals, sweat already glistening on skin in the desert heat.

There were no rules except that the fight was to the death, so they could start at any time, but they just stood there staring at each other.

Then the pirates got bored and a couple shoved them from behind, which was apparently what Castien had been waiting for as he used the momentum from the push to close the distance and slash out before Sam could recover.

He managed to twist out of the way to keep the blade from slicing open his throat, but searing pain shot through his arm as the blade cut it open just below the shoulder and blood was soon flowing down to drip off his hand.

There were a few cheers from the crowd, but it was greatly outnumbered by quiet murmuring.

The captain moved in to press his advantage, but this time Sam managed to deflect the blade and punch him in the face. The blow knocked him back, and Sam went to stab him in the gut, but Castien drove him back by slashing at his throat.

Numbness began to spread through Sam's left arm while a sense of drowsiness began to slow his reflexes. Was he really losing that much blood?

If he didn't win this fight soon, then he wouldn't at all.

The next time Castien came at him, he dropped to his knees as if to beg for his life, then when his opponent hesitated, he drove his knife up and into his gut.

The pain caused him to drop his knife, and Sam slowly stood to look the man in the eyes which had grown wide with pain and fear. He yanked the knife out, then stabbed him again, this time going up under the sternum and into the heart.

This time when he withdrew the knife, the man fell to the ground dead.

The crowd burst into cheers, Gary grabbed the captain's shirt and brought it before Sam who ripped the red skull and crossbones pin from the collar and held it up for all to see. They cheered all the louder and quickly began transferring their armbands back to the right.

"Break out the booze!" someone shouted as a junior pirate quickly applied a pressure bandage to Sam's wounded arm.

"NO!" the new captain shouted above the cheers, and silence instantly followed as they turned to stare at him. What kind of pirate wouldn't want to celebrate a victory like that?

"Prepare for attack!" he ordered, but no one moved.

He was considering grabbing them one at a time and shoving them towards the armory until they got the message, but then a short, heavyset man wearing a green armband stepped out of the crowd and walked up to him.

"Green Simon wishes to inform you that Black Lucius was killed sometime during the night by his lover. That faction is now controlled by Black Tempest," the man reported, then turned and walked away without waiting for a response.

That meant the attack which had been coming would be postponed or outright canceled while Tempest consolidated her power, and Sam looked at Gary as a smile slowly spread across his face.

"Okay, now we can party," he relented, and the whole base was soon filled with celebratory cheers and shouts as the crowd dispersed to spread the news.

The captaincy now belonged to Red Sam.

Heart of a Knight

Ordeos
Friday, August 17th, 2706
5:29 A.M.

A sweaty forearm proved useless in drying an equally damp forehead in the thick humidity, so Captain Wendy Ricine ignored the stinging in her eyes, focused on the track ahead, and increased her pace.

The faster speed made no difference.

No matter how loud the breeze blowing past her or her own breathing became; the voices continued to follow her.

Voices and screams.

The pain in her legs and chest was nothing compared to that of the still healing burns on her hands and arms, and the early morning darkness could not conceal the sight of her dead comrades.

She rounded the west end of the track and spotted a shadowy figure standing under the light by the storage bins. The person was watching her, but she looked away and increased her speed again in the hope that if she passed fast enough it would discourage them from trying to talk. She came out here this early to be alone and that's what she would be even if she had to pretend.

It didn't matter what she wanted because her training and experience forced her to examine details as she drew close and visibility improved.

She eventually recognized her commanding officer, someone she couldn't ignore, so she slowed and jogged up to him where she placed her right fist over her heart in salute.

He returned the salute, then stood there watching her as she endeavored to slow her breathing.

"Over half your unit died when the Vehlans surrounded you, but none would have survived if not for your efforts. You fought them off, then went back for the others, even going so far as to reach into burning vehicles to pull them out," he finally spoke.

She should have done more, should have been able to save the rest, but it was no use contradicting him so she remained silent.

"There are not many who would have kept going with the injuries you sustained, but when I arrived with reinforcements that's exactly what you were doing. I reported your actions to the Star Knights along with my recommendation for you to join their ranks, and they accepted it."

"It is my honor to serve and my only wish is to see an end to all threats to our people and the future we seek," she stated crisply.

"An attitude worthy of the knights. You will report to the training facility outside Arigean in one week. Your physical injuries will be healed by then," the major concluded. He transferred her new orders from his palco, the computer embedded in his left palm, to hers then walked away.

She watched him go, then grabbed the towel from her bin and used it to dry the sweat still dripping off her. The sky was just starting to brighten as she finished and tossed it over a shoulder before walking away from the track.

All her muscles ached from the exertion, but somehow she felt better leaving than when she had arrived, as if a great weight had been lifted from her shoulders.

She had a purpose, and was finally going to the best place to see it through.

Monday, August 27th, 2706
9:58 A.M.

The itch was maddening, but Wendy refused to even wrinkle her nose in an effort to clear it and concentrated on maintaining perfect posture. It had been two hours since the instructors had called the cadets to attention only to do nothing but stand there and watch them, but she would stand here for as long as it took.

They were yet to receive their training uniforms, so each of them had reported to the field in full dress uniform which made for an interesting collage with the mix of colors and styles from the different services. The dark green suit jacket and black dress of Wendy's infantry uniform was nearly unbearable in the summer sun but the fabric breathed well enough to dry any sweat before it could stain the outfit.

The three instructors standing at the front of the formation suddenly snapped to attention and Knight Commander Grellin, the training facility director, walked on to the parade grounds between them and the cadets and came to a stop at the center. He surveyed them with zero expression on his face and seemed to make eye contact with each and every one of the hundred prospects arranged before him.

When he came to Wendy, she did not meet his gaze but instead focused on the horizon.

"I have one piece of advice for you. Forget everything you have accomplished to this point because it does not matter. It earned you a recommendation to join our ranks, but we don't care. You are nothing until we say otherwise," Grellin announced as he continued his scrutiny.

Everything Wendy had done was always out of necessity, not out of any sense of personal pride, so his denigration did little to affect her.

"You get one chance to become a Star Knight. If you fail this training regimen, future recommendations will be ignored and there is no applying for a second attempt. Failure for a knight could lead to the emperor's death and the destruction of our nation. There is no margin of error for us."

Failure was not something Wendy tolerated either, so this only told her she was in the right place.

"The nature of this training is considered top secret. You are forbidden to talk to anyone outside the knights of your experiences here. Violate this command and the consequences will be severe."

She rarely talked to people anyway, so that wouldn't be a problem.

"When this assembly is dismissed, you will go to the bunkhouse where you will be assigned a room. After that is finished, you will be free to spend the rest of the day and evening as you choose. If you wish to go into town, transportation will be provided to you."

The knight commander scanned the formation again, his face just as expressionless as before, then he finally nodded to one of the instructors before turning and leaving the way he had come.

The instructor pointed out the bunkhouse on the west end of the facility, then dismissed them. They saluted with right fist to heart, grabbed their bags from off the ground, then most headed for their accommodations but some ran towards the lavatories on the side of the field.

A flicker of light caught Wendy's eye, and she looked back to the front of the field where she noticed one of the instructors tapping at his palco's holographic display as he looked between it and those rushing to relieve themselves.

She quickly looked away and pretended not to have noticed as she hustled to obey her instructions.

7:57 P.M.

After the cadets were given their room assignments and dismissed for the day, Wendy had left her bag on the bed against the room's left wall then gone and thoroughly explored the base. She noticed most of the others doing the same, but chose to avoid them and keep to herself.

Once she was fully acquainted with her surroundings, she had returned to the room and set to work unpacking. She was hanging her general uniform in the wardrobe at the end of her bed when a black-haired woman in a fleet officer's uniform entered, opened the bag on the other bed, then began pulling out the clothes and putting them away.

"I saw you around the base today. It looks like we're the only two women in this class. I'm Commander Trudi Azante," she introduced herself.

"Captain Wendy Ricine."

"Why did you join the knights?"

"I was recommended."

"We all were, but it was still our choice to come. I'm curious why you want to be here."

"This is where I can best serve our people by protecting our emperor and destroying his enemies," Wendy answered with the hope it would end the conversation.

It didn't.

"I want to establish our right to be here. Men and women are considered equal in every part of the empire, except in the Star Knights. The men seem to think they're the only ones capable of enduring the difficulties, and I'm determined to prove them wrong. It took me longer to get recommended than I wanted, but tracking down and capturing a spy finally convinced them," Trudi explained.

It was no secret that even while women were allowed to join the knights they were presented with greater challenges in an effort to cause them to fail or quit, but Wendy thought it a poor and possibly even dangerous reason to join merely to prove a point. She had no desire to argue, however; so she said nothing and finished her task by folding her bag and placing it on the bottom shelf of the cabinet.

She unfolded a white t-shirt and a pair of grey sweats and laid them out on the bed, then glanced at her roommate to see that she had already changed into a sangria colored dress and was now sitting on the edge of her bed pulling on a pair of black ankle boots.

"I'm going into town for the evening. Do you want to come?" she asked after standing up, but Wendy merely shook her head no after which Trudi walked out to finally leave her in peace.

She changed into the sweats and shirt, hung her uniform in the wardrobe, then grabbed her bag of toiletries and headed for the washroom, grateful for the choice of socks when her feet hit the cold, hard floor in the common room.

There was a knight by the exit who glanced her way and looked her up and down, but he didn't do anything so she just continued on her way.

The building's only restroom was empty when she entered, and she went to the nearest sink to wash her face and clean her teeth, having decided to shower in the morning.

Another cadet came in shortly after she started, and she watched him in the mirror as he glanced at her then went into a stall, closing the door behind him.

She was almost finished when he came back out and took the sink next to her to wash his hands.

"I noticed you a couple times today, and you were always by yourself," he commented.

"My purpose is to serve the empire, not make friends," she responded curtly.

"The empire is best served when we work together as a team, and a team works better when its members know one another."

"We will learn all we need to know during the training."

"I see no reason why we can't start now."

"I do," she countered, then placed her items back in the bag and left.

He caught up with her in the common room and grabbed her by the arm.

"Don't ignore me. We are all in this together, no matter your personal feelings. Now come join me for some fun in town while we have the option," he jeered.

She looked at the hand gripping her arm, then up into his bright blue eyes and stared into them.

He glared back, but his resolve quickly withered under her gaze and he let go of her. She continued staring until he scoffed and left, passing by the knight Wendy had noticed earlier who she now realized was watching them with intense interest.

He watched the male cadet leave, then looked back at her and continued to watch without saying anything. There was nothing she had to say to him, so she simply went back to her room, put away her things, and got into bed.

11:27 P.M.

The sound of a door handle turning woke Wendy, and she opened her eyes to see her roommate trudge into the room and collapse on her bed without bothering to change her disheveled clothes.

So wasteful, Wendy thought, but it was her choice if the woman wanted to throw away her time and energy like that. It wasn't Wendy's concern, so she closed her eyes and went back to sleep.

Tuesday, August 28th, 2706
7:00 A.M.

The cadets were assembled on a dirt field enclosed by a metal fence, clad in their training uniforms of a tight gray shirt tucked into thick khaki colored pants which were themselves tucked into black combat boots. Knight Commander Grellin was not present, but Knight Captain Uzin, his second, stood atop a platform on the other side of the fence while eight other knights were spaced out around the perimeter.

"Only true warriors can become knights, and a warrior is always physically, mentally, and emotionally prepared for whatever may happen. We do not waste resources training the weak, so our first task is to eliminate half this class," he revealed.

There were a few surprised whispers from the assembly, but they quickly dissipated.

"This is the melee where you will fight one another until only one half remains standing. The only rule is that you do not attempt to kill one another, but be aware that death is a possibility we accept and for which you should be prepared."

The knight captain looked over them, occasionally stopping to scrutinize a particular cadet, but he passed right over Wendy. Such a test was a surprise, but her determination did not waver.

When he was finished with his survey, Uzin drew his pistol and pointed it into the air.

"You will begin when I fire. Do not hesitate."

He stayed that way for what felt like minutes, carefully watching them as if awaiting a certain reaction.

The man to Wendy's left began to fidget, but she and the others around her remained calm.

Then the gun went off, and the man to her left turned and tried to grab her, but she jumped forward, spun to the side, and delivered a hand chop to the back of his neck. He fell face first into the dirt and didn't get up.

She saw two others grappling with each other and tripped one of them by hooking her foot behind his ankle which caused both of them to fall with one on top the other.

A kick to the ribs knocked the one on top to the ground, and she followed through by stomping on the other one's stomach. He doubled up in pain, but the first one grabbed her ankle and pulled, causing her to fall backward.

The impact forced the air from her lungs, but she managed to hold her head up enough to avoid injury. Her opponent scrambled over the man between them and went to jump on top of her, but she punched him in the side of the head then knocked him out with an elbow to the face when he fell at her side.

She jumped up again and looked down at the man still holding his stomach, but he shook his head when he saw her looking so she left him alone.

A shadow approached from behind her, so she spun around and instantly recognized the blue eyes staring back at her, this time filled with a nasty glee.

"You can't ignore me now."

Her only response was to raise her fists and assume a fighting stance.

His smile transformed into a scowl, and he threw a left hook at her face, but she blocked it and countered with a kick to the midsection, but it only connected with air when he twisted out of the way.

They broke apart and squared off again, then he kicked her in the shin and followed with a punch to the face when she involuntarily dropped her hands.

The punch was strong enough to spin her head around, but she shifted her weight to her left foot and used the energy to twist her whole body and deliver a roundhouse kick to his face.

This knocked him off-balance and she drove her right elbow into his back which finally drove him to the ground.

He rolled over and kicked at her, but she had already stepped to his side and now she delivered a powerful kick to his face, causing him to scream and grab his nose as blood gushed over his hands.

Gunshots from all around the field cut through the yells and impacts and she looked at Uzin to see him signaling a stop.

The fighting noises subsided, and she looked around to see half of the cadets on the ground either unconscious or in too much pain to get up while the rest were bruised and bloody but still standing.

She looked down at her last opponent who had overcome his pain enough to lie still and stare at her with intense hate, and considered saying something to him about how he'll never bother her again, but decided he wasn't worth it and just walked away instead.

"Those of you still standing, relocate to the gym. An instructor will meet you there to discuss what you did wrong here. Everyone else who can still hear me, collect your belongings and leave this base immediately. You will never be knights," Uzin announced, and Wendy broke into a jog with the rest.

"I'm glad you made it. We'll make a stronger point if we both make it through," a voice said from behind her after she vaulted the fence, and she looked to the right to see Trudi come up beside her.

It was pointless to make a point, but Wendy stayed silent and set her mind on the next task.

Friday, November 30th, 2706
3:27 P.M.

A quick inhale followed the sharp pain which shot through Wendy's arm as she grabbed the rope, but she grit her teeth and pulled herself up another few inches.

The fracture from last month had yet to heal due to having received no treatment, but her training continued. A knight's mission had to be completed no matter the personal consequences, and no less was expected of them in training.

There were only three options: succeed, fail, or die. Whichever one was the result, the injury and the pain it caused would cease to matter.

One more pull brought her to the top, then she grabbed hold of the wooden planks and pulled herself up onto the platform. As soon as she had her feet under her again, she dashed to the table on the right, grabbed one of the four red and grey pennant flags, then ran down ten meters of zig-zag stairs on the other side and presented it to Knight Captain Uzin.

He took the flag, set it with six others on the dark wood table next to him, then jerked his head towards the other cadets already standing behind him. She saluted with her right fist over heart, then hustled to the line and took her position standing at attention at the end.

Three months of training culminated in this final obstacle course. She was hurt, tired, and covered in sweat-streaked filth, but she had made it this far and it was almost over. She would be a knight.

Two more cadets soon followed, the first with fresh blood running down the left side of his face from a reopened gash on his forehead and the other limping from a broken foot. They presented their flags, then took their place on the line. The next one took a little longer, but finally Trudi bounded down the stairs and turned in the last flag.

She smiled at Wendy as she passed, then took her place at the end.

"Congratulations. The ten of you have passed this test and still have a chance to serve with us. Five did not, and will never know the honor of being a knight. Get yourselves cleaned up and report to the assembly hall at seventeen hundred. Dismissed!" Uzin declared.

The cadets saluted, turned as one, then jogged over the soggy ground back to the barracks.

5:01 P.M.

"One-hundred of you started this training program. Ten of you remain. Some final proof of your worthiness to be called knights yet remains, but you have earned yourselves a break," Knight Commander Grellin announced from behind the podium in the cavernous assembly hall, his face as expressionless as ever.

The cadets stood at attention in a single row, and not one of them offered any reaction to his words.

"Put on your best training uniform and report to the main garage by nineteen hundred hours. You are to spend the evening in town, then report back to the dropoff point by twenty-three hundred. This base will be closed to you until then. Dismissed," Grellin told them, then turned and walked away with the other instructors following.

"Why would they send us out of here before the training is finished?" one cadet wondered aloud.

"It's likely to let us relieve stress so we can face the final tests with clear minds," another responded.

"The reason doesn't concern me. I'm not going to waste this chance," Trudi commented.

If anything more was said, Wendy didn't hear because she was already on her way out of the room.

Arigean
9:34 P.M.

The music was deafening, the strobing lights headache inducing, and the crowd was so thick a person couldn't walk without bumping into everyone around them, but the rain prevented Wendy from going for a walk and there wasn't anywhere else to go in this town, so she did her best to tolerate the situation as she waited to return to base.

Strict sobriety laws, regardless of circumstance, kept the club from serving hard alcohol and forced the proprietors to hold their customers to a limit, but that didn't stop people from dancing and socializing.

It all seemed like a waste of time and energy to Wendy who had chosen a spot in the most isolated corner she could find and just watched the activity. The other cadets were also in the club, but she had lost track of them some time ago.

"It seems a shame for a beautiful woman such as yourself to be sitting here all by herself, especially without a drink," a man commented as he slid into the booth and set a glass with ice and an amber liquid in front of her.

"I'm not interested," she rebuffed while barely sparing him a glance.

"These drinks cost me two hours of allotment, so I think that's worth a little conversation," the man insisted as he took a sip from his own glass.

She looked at him, but did not speak or reach for the offered drink. He was a few years older than her with dark hair, but the shadows hid the rest of his features. He was handsome enough from what she could see, but she still wasn't interested. Nothing could be allowed to distract from her calling.

"I see that you are a knight in training. How is that going?" he asked.

She did not answer.

"What did you do to get recommended?"

No response.

"Why did you choose to join?"

Nothing.

"Are you going to say anything at all?"

A flat stare was all he got.

"I see. You're not even a knight yet, but you already think you're better than the rest of us," he challenged, then gave her a pointed look as if he expected that would get a rise out of her.

It didn't.

He sighed, took another sip, then set down his glass as he smiled like he'd just had the best idea ever.

"I retired from military service before earning a recommendation for the knights, but I managed to accomplish a few noteworthy things in my time. I wouldn't mind having the chance to become a knight myself, but I have no idea what's required. Suppose you tell me about the training so I can decide if it is something I want to do."

"I will tell you nothing. Now leave before you come to regret ever having noticed me," she threatened.

He chuckled as if he didn't believe her, but his mirth quickly turned to fear when he looked into her eyes and realized that she was indeed willing to hurt him.

"I'll go find someone who isn't dead inside," he jeered, then picked up his drink and stood up.

She watched him until he disappeared into the crowd, then got up and went outside.

The rain was preferable to this nonsense.

Saturday, December 1st, 2706
8:00 A.M.

The door swung open as Wendy's hand still hung in the air after knocking, and she was greeted by an armored knight, his or her identity concealed by the helmet's faceplate.

This person stepped aside and swept their arm towards the room, so she went through the door. She noticed that the knight was also armed with a rifle on the back and pistol at the hip, but she confidently stepped into the center of the room and saluted when she saw Knight Commander Grellin.

There was not a single piece of furniture or wall decoration and every surface was bright white. The blurred reflections also told her the surfaces were coated in a smooth, non-porous material.

On either side of Grellin stood an instructor, and to Ricine's right stood two more knights in armor with Trudi in between clad in a black dress with white stripes on the outside of the legs and a black jacket, the formal uniform of a fleet officer.

The instructors and Grellin were also in their formal grey uniforms with red belts, the only uniform available to knights aside from the ceremonial robes, but Wendy had merely donned a fresh training uniform.

"Cadet Ricine. What activities did you perform while on leave yesterday evening?" Grellin asked.

"I ate dinner at a restaurant, sat at the local club for approximately one hour, then walked around the town until it was time to return."

"Did you speak to anyone?"

"As little as possible, sir."

"You would swear under oath that you did not reveal details about this program to anyone?"

"Yes, sir."

The commander scrutinized her for a moment, then nodded to the knight at the door behind her. She didn't turn around, but she heard the door open and someone enter the room who came up to stand behind her to the right.

"Did this individual reveal any information when you questioned her?" Grellin inquired of the new arrival.

"No, sir."

She recognized the voice as belonging to the man from the club last night, and tensed up as she fought to keep her surprise from showing.

"Did you continue to observe her for the rest of the leave period?"

"Yes, sir."

He had followed her after she left! How did she not notice!

"Was she in contact with anyone else before returning to the rendezvous?"

"Negative."

"You're dismissed," Grellin concluded. A sharp rustling indicated the man saluted, then the door opened and closed again and he was gone.

The commander ordered Wendy to stand at rest, then walked up to stand between her and Trudi whom the former noticed for the first time was watching the proceedings with wide eyes on the brink of tearing up.

"The man who questioned you in regards to your training is one of our agents, and your interaction with him was to gauge your trustworthiness. Cadet Ricine passed this test; Cadet Azante did not," Grellin revealed, his tone dropping at the end.

The condemned woman started to say something, but the commander shut her down with a single look and she shut her mouth tight.

He then stared her in the eyes as he pulled out his pistol, and her eyes locked on the weapon and grew even wider, but instead of using it he turned to face Wendy and held it out to her grip first.

"The penalty for this infraction is death. You have been chosen to carry out this sentence summarily," he told her.

She looked at the gun, but did not take it. She had killed many people in her time as a soldier, but never another imperial. Now they wanted her to execute her own roommate, going against everything she believed about trust between comrades.

But the rules were broken, they were all told this would be the punishment, and her commanding officer had issued an order, so she took the gun and aimed at the traitor's face.

"Please don't do this," Trudi begged, tears welling up in her hazel eyes.

"You brought this on yourself," Wendy scolded, then pulled the trigger. The shot slammed the woman into the wall behind her, then she slowly slid to the floor after which Wendy returned the pistol to its owner.

"Welcome to the Star Knights, Initiate Ricine."

Heart of a Champion

OES Dragon's Breath
Tuesday, December 4th, 2706
9:01 A.M.

"See to it that all duties are properly distributed between returning and new personnel," Legion Commander Max Canza ordered upon entering the tactical center with his second-in-command, both of them in the black uniforms of fleet officers with the red across the chest and yellow stripes over the shoulders. The other man took his place at the appropriate console and began his work, but it was clear that his thoughts were elsewhere.

"We are stronger than ever and the Vehlans are falling before us with no hope of stopping us. Our new emperor is doing extremely well, especially given his young age," Legion Captain Tony Farra commented.

The commander said nothing as he focused on ensuring the recently conquered Grilke system was fully secure, unwilling to trust their position and safety to the apathy of its residents. Farra could be overly optimistic, but he was a true believer in the Ordonian cause and such people always had their uses.

"Incoming communication from Ordeos, Legion Commander," Communications reported from the bridge. He told them to relay it to the tactical center, then faced the main screen on the wall and came to attention while Farra remained out of sight behind his workstation.

"What are my orders?" he asked when Knight Commander Lanze appeared onscreen in his grey uniform suit. A Star Knight giving orders to regular military was an abomination, but Canza made a point to maintain his dispassionate exterior that revealed no trace of the disgust he felt.

As the emperor's elite security service, the knights were outside the military's chain of command, but since the primary had died in battle with the secondaries dismissed from their positions shortly afterward, Emperor Johan was using them to relay his orders.

"A squadron will arrive shortly to garrison the Grilke system in your stead. You are to take your legion and destroy the Vehlan fleet stationed at Narsol," Lanze dictated.

There was a scarcely audible gasp from Farra's location behind the legion commander, but he offered no reaction of his own.

"That fleet is their primary defense for their homeworld and surrounding systems, and the system contains many military installations. It is impossible for a single legion to invade it."

It was also deep behind enemy lines, but reaching it wasn't a concern, only what to do once he arrived.

"Your objective is not to invade the system, only to destroy the fleet by any means at your disposal. Do not attempt to seize the territory."

"Understood. Is there anything else?"

"Return to your home base when finished. That is all," Lanze concluded, then cut the connection.

"We don't have the numbers or firepower to challenge that fleet!" Farra blurted after stepping into the open.

"Prepare for the changeover. I want the legion ready to debark within three hours of our relief's arrival," Canza ordered as he approached an auxiliary screen to the left of the center walkway.

He called up the Narsol system and displayed all information on its military assets, filling the screen with blue dots and a column of green text on the right.

It was an impressive collection of ships and troops, but success was possible and he wouldn't settle for anything less.

Saturday, December 8th, 2706
4:32 P.M.

The bridge's main screen showed three green, four-pointed stars against a map grid rapidly approaching the Narsol system as Legion Commander Canza watched from the captain's chair, his hands resting in his lap and eyes intently watching.

"Attack squadrons report ready, sir," Farra relayed the report, and Canza nodded to signal them to proceed.

Two of the squadrons came out of hyperspace and engaged the Vehlan ships already waiting for them thanks to their early warning system. The mass of red icons of various shapes nearly enveloped the two stars, but both of them managed to break through.

One turned back and maintained engagement with the first set of defenders, but the second continued on and headed for the planet Narsol itself.

More defenders broke orbit to intercept and quickly stopped the intruders a safe distance away from the planet.

Canza watched as his outnumbered forces began to crumble under the enthusiastic defense, but patiently bided his time.

"Now," he finally said.

The third squadron bypassed the fighting and entered normal space dangerously close to the planet, but they pulled off the maneuver without incident. The larger ships opened fire on the remaining defenders in orbit as half a dozen bomber squadrons descended into the atmosphere with their fighter escorts.

Ground-based fighters scrambled in response, but only managed to stop four of the squadrons. The remaining two made it through and destroyed their targets, one of which was the oldest military academy in the entire Vehlan Union, then all of them sped away with the defenders hot on their tail. The bombers and fighters docked with their host craft, then all Ordonian forces fled the system.

The red icons on Canza's screen disappeared when his ships entered hyperspace, but nearly half of them reappeared seconds later in pursuit of those who had dared attack them.

6:59 P.M.

"Prepare for battle," the legion commander ordered as the ships approached his location. The lights dimmed as power was transferred to the combat systems, and half the main screen changed to a visual view.

The rest of his fleet awaited the action near a red dwarf star with no planets not far from the Narsol system. Since the Vehlans were stretched thin in the war, they were only patrolling it every few days with the belief the imperials would never get this far into their territory anyway.

Understandable, but foolish.

His attack ships appeared and immediately consolidated into a tight defensive formation, then the Vehlans showed up and surrounded them, but didn't fire. They likely intended to demand their surrender.

"Execute," Canza ordered.

Two-thirds of his fleet suddenly dropped out of hyperspace on either side of the enemy as the Dragon's Breath led the remaining third away from the star and closed the remaining gap.

He wasn't going to ask them to surrender.

"Fire at will."

The visual display lit up with the white light of plasma bolts and the blue of missiles as the Ordonians rained death on their enemy, then red joined the spectacle as the Vehlans returned fire but to a far lesser extent. They desperately tried to turn for a better firing position, but it was too late for that and soon orange fireballs were added to the color show.

When most of the enemy ships were destroyed, Canza ordered the three attack squadrons plus one more from the fleet to stay behind and finish the job then had the rest regroup and set course for Narsol.

"Do you still think we can't do this?" he remarked to Farra after the display changed to the milky colors of hyperspace.

"No. I now believe this will be one of the most spectacular victories of this war."

Thursday, January 31st, 2707
7:49 A.M.

The royal palace loomed over the legion commander clad in full dress uniform as he walked up the tree-lined marble path, its red stone and wood walls and colonnaded entrance filling him with pride and satisfaction although he dared not show this to the armored knights on patrol. His service to the empire had not gone unnoticed and now he would have the opportunity to do even more.

He ascended the twelve steps, entered via the wide open doors, then passed through the security station after which he was told to wait in a side lobby.

A herald dressed in a dark yellow suit came through the wooden door on the other side a couple minutes later and told him to follow. They entered a large hallway where ten armored Star Knights stood guard, one on each door leading to the lobby and four on either side of the currently open four and a half meter tall doors.

The two of them traversed the thick red carpet between fourteen pairs of gold columns, in between each of which stood more knights, and approached the throne dais where another legion commander already stood with his hands clasped behind his back. His dress uniform with its dark green jacket, red shirt, and black pants with the red stripe on the outside mirrored Canza's own.

When he came up beside the other man, Canza recognized him as Raz Vinton, the commander of the invasion of Vehla who had managed to secure nearly the entire planet only to suffer a horrendous defeat upon attacking the final stronghold.

"Do you know this man's identity?" Emperor Johan asked from atop the dais after the herald introduced Canza. His four personal guards with their ceremonial armor and shields stood at each corner, but the empress was not present.

The emperor normally wore a set of robes unique to his office, but today he was dressed in the royal military uniform with its dark red pants, double-breasted black jacket with brass buttons, and black combat boots. There was also a pistol holstered at his right hip.

This was not a good sign.

"Yes, Majesty."

"Are you aware of his recent failure?"

"I am."

"Do you know how many soldiers died in that attack?"

"The exact number is yet to be reported, sire."

"The reason for that is because we are still recovering their bodies from the field while avoiding enemy fire, but we know that this man sent over twenty-thousand to their deaths."

That was the number Canza had heard, but there was no question in the last statement so he did not respond.

The emperor looked from him to the other legion commander, then drew his pistol and with perfect aim shot the man in the face.

Canza did not flinch at the gunshot nor the sound of the body hitting the floor and kept a steady gaze on his liege.

"I am placing you in command of the Vehlan siege. You will conduct yourself with the same excellence as your last mission," the emperor decreed as he holstered his weapon.

"I understand, Majesty," Canza responded with a bow.

"I will not be disappointed again. You're dismissed."

Pirate Honor

Altaius
Green Command Center
Saturday, January 4th, 2708
11:03 A.M.

"I wasn't expecting a visit from you so soon," Captain Turley, aka Green Simon, commented from behind his desk.

"There's a job I need you to do, and I suggest you give it your full attention," Red Sam responded as he marched up to the desk.

"You seized control of all the pirate factions less than a day ago, and already you're strutting around making demands. I'm not sure I could ever be that cocky."

Sam smiled as he leaned forward and placed his hands on the desk.

"Black Tempest underestimated my power, and my resolve, and paid the price. I've proven what I can do, and have no need, or desire, to be subtle."

"You wouldn't even be a captain if it weren't for my help. I've earned a certain respect no matter how much power you gain."

"I paid your price in full. The slate is clean, and I will treat you the same as any other captain. You need to respect *that*."

His eyes narrowed as Simon studied the man who fancied himself king of all pirates. Perhaps it was the wrong decision to help him in his mutiny against the previous red captain, but he couldn't risk that faction becoming too weak and there was no way to predict that thousands of ex-union soldiers would one day join him.

There wasn't anything he could do about it now, but one day he would once again be master of his own fate.

"What is it you want?" he finally asked. His guest straightened up and placed his hands behind his back before responding.

"Find and eliminate any moles within our ranks. I've ordered the other captains to allow you free access to their records, and I will do the same."

"How do your new allies feel about 'eliminating' people?"

"My allies are my concern. Yours is to do your job, or we'll all be facing Ordonian execution squads soon."

"If it's the Ordonians you're worried about, you should know that not even I can identify an undercover Star Knight. Even if I could, I'd never be able to take him out covertly."

"The Star Knights have little interest in us, certainly not enough to plant an operative. It's the civilian law enforcement agencies we have to worry about."

"Is my reward for doing this simply to continue living?"

"That hardly seems like a simple thing to me, but no, that is not to be all of it. I will pay you a bounty for each spy you unmask, and if you can prove to my satisfaction that you have found all of them, I will reduce your tribute to me," Red Sam explained.

"So generous," Turley responded dryly. The other captain gave him an annoyed look, but chose to leave instead of engaging in further banter.

Friday, January 10th, 2708
1:52 P.M.

"You are a member of the security firm Whitman Investigations. Your assignment is to spy on the Orange pirates with the intent of finding and apprehending those responsible for the recent raids against three Merchant's Interest corporations," Green Simon stated. The man standing before him went visibly pale at the accusation, and struggled to utter a defense.

"Don't bother trying to deny it. I never say such things without being sure of their accuracy."

"Why are you talking to me instead of Orange David?" the man, Pirate Benson, asked.

"If I report you to Captain Saxen, he will either send you home or kill you, but I'd prefer to put you to work for us."

"Doing what?"

"You will transfer to my command where you will receive a promotion to the rank of sergeant, and I will tell you what information to report to your firm. Your new duties will be to supply me with intel on the Merchant's Interest, as well as the other pirate factions should I see the need.

"Your promotion here will come with higher pay, and will also earn you a promotion in your firm. One day you will return to that life, so I'm sure you can see the benefits in that," the captain explained.

"Not if they learn I was bought out by a pirate."

"That will never happen."

"What if I refuse?"

"Then I report you to Orange David and let him deal with you as he sees fit."

The two of them fell silent as Benson considered the situation.

"You give me your word that one day I'll be allowed to return home?"

"Your company will recall you one day, and if we did anything to prevent your return, it would bring increased scrutiny down on us, something which no pirate wants. It is in my best interest to let you go at that time, provided you never reveal the truth regarding the time you spent in my employ."

"Then I accept your offer."

"Go get your things. I will contact Orange David to apprise him of the transfer, and will see to it he doesn't give you any trouble," Simon told him, then turned his attention to his computer, leaving the pirate to show himself out.

The door hadn't yet swung closed when Lieutenant Pakston pushed it open again and hastily approached the desk.

"We've discovered another one!"

"In what faction, and who sent him?" the captain asked, giving the man his full attention.

"Red, and the Ordeon Empire."

"An imperial agent in Sam's own ranks. A somewhat amusing prospect," Simon responded, then paused a moment to savor the irony.

A multitude of scenarios ran through his mind at lightspeed, many of which left him with a significant advantage over the arrogant imbecile.

"Bring him to me," he ordered.

"I can't. He was sent out on a raiding party yesterday."

"You let him leave this planet!"

"The connection was found and confirmed only a few minutes ago."

"Prepare my ship for immediate departure. We have to get to him before he can meet with a contact."

Culture Blend
Monday, January 13th, 2708
7:02 P.M.

"Stow your armbands," Simon ordered as his group neared its destination. This particular town was a popular destination for criminals of all types since the locals only cared about crimes committed within its limits, but their mission required them to avoid the attention of more than just law enforcement.

"What's the plan?" Pakston asked as he slid the green band off his right arm and pocketed it.

"We're a group of friends out for a night on the town, not pirates or soldiers."

"Got it."

"Not exactly the kind of place you'd expect to find an imperial, or a red for that matter," another pirate commented as the bar came within view.

"Making it the perfect place for someone working both camps to hide," Pakston responded. The group's pace slowed as they instinctively surveyed the building for entrances, exits, and overall defensibility.

The place was a wreck with missing wall coverings, cracked windows, and a sagging roof. Looking at it made one question how the place remained standing, but ironically, it was probably built that way for tourist appeal. That also meant the floor plan would be standard and easy to plan around.

"You two, cover the back. You two get the front. If you see him leave, shoot him dead. Pakston, you're with me," Simon dealt out the assignments, then walked off without waiting for a response.

He timed it so that a group of rowdy college students made it to the door before him, then he entered right on their heels and quickly sauntered into a dark corner where he found an empty table and took a seat.

While he scanned the room from this perspective, Pakston casually made his way to the bar where he ordered a couple drinks. He leaned on the counter looking bored, but was carefully studying each face the whole time.

It wasn't long before Simon spotted two men at a small table on the other side of the room, speaking earnestly with untouched drinks on the table between them. He couldn't make out their faces, and the sight wasn't necessarily uncommon in this environment, but something told him this was the man he was after.

He caught Pakston's attention and jerked his head in the direction of the table in question, after which the lieutenant collected the freshly arrived drinks and made his way over to the captain by a route that allowed him a good look at the two men.

"That's him," he confirmed as he took a seat.

"Then that has to be his handler. We can't let either one of them leave here alive," Simon observed before taking a sip.

"If we follow them and kill them in an alley somewhere, the Ordonians will investigate and we'll be just as screwed."

Simon nodded in agreement, then sat in silent observation of his targets and the room as a whole while he considered his options.

"There will be an imperial investigation if those two are the only ones who die," he finally commented, eliciting a confused look from his lieutenant. He explained his plan, after which Pakston downed the rest of his drink in one gulp before standing up and loudly proclaiming he had to pee.

"There's going to be a lot of people running out of here in a moment. Keep your eyes peeled, and make sure the spy doesn't escape," Simon ordered the men standing watch outside via the comlink hidden in his ear.

As Pakston stumbled through the room, Simon got up and moved towards the spy's table, getting close enough to strike but carefully staying in the shadows.

When he was in position, Pakston tripped and fell into a man who had been loudly arguing with his friends, pushing him onto the table and spilling booze all over the place.

"Hey! Watch where you're going!" the man proclaimed as he pushed himself off the table and to his feet.

"Nobody talks to me like that!" Pakston shouted, then shoved the guy so hard he fell onto the table and slid across to fall onto the floor on the other side.

His three friends shot to their feet and one threw a punch, but the pirate deftly dodged it, picked up a glass bottle in the same motion, and swung it around to “accidentally” break it over the head of an innocent bystander.

By this time the altercation had caught the attention of the spy and his handler, and they rose to their feet as it grew into a full-scale brawl. Simon slid his combat knife from its hidden holster at his waist, then quickly closed the distance and plunged it into the spy's chest.

He pushed the man away, leaving the knife in him, and turned to deal with the other one, but was stopped by the table slamming into his gut.

He shoved the table aside and squared off against his opponent who now had a knife out in position to thrust forward, but another patron fell into him and bought Simon the time he needed to grab a bottle from another table and break it on the edge.

The Ordonian agent stabbed towards his gut, but he dodged to the right and tripped him, sending him sprawling onto the floor. Simon jumped on his back intending to slash his throat, but the agent managed to elbow him in the face and knock him to the floor as well.

Someone tripped over Simon and fell onto the agent, and the pirate used the distraction to shove his broken bottle into the agent's throat.

He then pried the knife out of the agent's hand, got back on his feet, and stabbed it into the back of the nearest person.

The mission accomplished, he fought his way over to Pakston at the center of the brawl, grabbed the battered pirate out of the clutches of those he had provoked and practically dragged him out of the establishment.

“I want a raise,” he muttered after they rejoined the others and were on their way to the spaceport.

“I'll think about it.”

Altaius
Wednesday, January 15th,2708
6:24 P.M.

Four Dead and Eleven Seriously Injured in Bar Riot. Instigators Unknown.

"I hope it was worth it," Pakston remarked after reading the headline on his palco.

"We prevented the Ordonians from learning about our new situation, didn't we?" Simon retorted.

"Yeah, but I'm not sure I see the point. Why did I have to nearly get myself killed to protect Red Sam? We could have let the Ordonians get rid of him and you would probably be the one in charge now."

"That isn't something I want. I prefer to work behind the scenes where one is less likely to get shot in the face. Even if I did want Sam's position, I wouldn't get it that way. At best, the factions would simply go their separate ways again, but the more likely outcome is the Ordonians would wipe all of us out."

"You know that's exactly where Sam is leading us, right?"

"They'll come for us eventually, one way or the other. Now that the Vehlan Union is gone, there's nothing to stop them from imposing their will on everyone. Whether we like it or not, our best hope for survival now lies in working together."

"So I guess we really do work for the reds now? I was hoping you were just playing along long enough to find a way out."

"That's exactly what I'm doing, but as pirates our first priority is surviving when everyone wants to imprison or kill us. No one knows what the future holds, and all we can do is get by as best we can with the knowledge we do have."

See more from this author on Amazon!

Acknowledgements

Thank you to my dad for his continued support and encouragement on this never-ending journey of mine.

Special thanks to artist Calley Dunnihoo who created the first cover and has stuck with me on this journey from the first edition to the current revision.

And to all my friends who tolerate my rambling on about non-existent worlds and my constant requests for feedback.

About the author

An active imagination has been one of Dodge's defining attributes for as long as he can remember, with its creations often seeming more real to him than the world in which he lived. Upon discovering a talent and affinity for the written word, he began writing stories for fun at first, then eventually decided to make it more than a hobby. This has taught him to control his wandering mind while also providing an escape for him and others.

Born in northern Illinois, his family moved to southern Missouri shortly afterward where he currently lives with his two cats Merry and Pippin who provide comfort and drive him crazy multiple times a day. He rides a motorcycle, exercises regularly, and trains in Brazilian Jiu-Jitsu when possible.

Also by Dodge Merrin

Follow me on Amazon!

Embers of Hope Science Fiction Miniseries

<u>Triumphant Empire</u>

Available through Amazon & KU.

Revolution

Available through Amazon.

Total War

Available through Amazon.

Brink of Extinction

Available through Amazon.

See Also

Humble Glory

Available through Amazon & KU.

www.ingramcontent.com/pod-product-compliance
Lightning Source LLC
LaVergne TN
LVHW090606110826
845146LV00001B/281

* 9 7 9 8 9 9 0 9 0 7 9 6 6 *